MISSING OR DEAD

Missing or Dead

A Patrick Dawlish Mystery

John Creasey *writing as*
Gordon Ashe

This edition published in 2025 by Open Road Integrated Media, Inc.
180 Maiden Lane
New York, NY 10038
www.openroadmedia.com

MISSING OR DEAD

CHAPTER ONE

REQUEST

The smoking-room of the Carilon Club was so vast that it dwarfed the members; even the largest of these, whose name was Patrick Dawlish. In a recumbent position with his fair head resting on the back of a huge arm-chair and his legs stretched straight in front of him, Dawlish looked massive. His eyes were closed and his mouth was slightly slack, because he was in that golden state, neither awake nor really asleep.

Upon this peaceful scene came a dark-clad boy with curly hair and rosy cheeks, a pretty picture of a lad, who was older than he looked.

'Excuse me, sir,' whispered the cherub.

Dawlish opened one eye.

'There is a gentleman to see you, sir.'

'Oh,' said Dawlish. He raised his head. 'Pity. What's the time?'

'Three-fifteen, sir.'

'Then I suppose I ought to be up and doing,' said Dawlish. 'Who is it?'

'He didn't give his name, sir.'

'Oh,' said Dawlish. 'Where is he?'

'In the waiting-room, sir.'

Dawlish nodded, and stood up. The swift ease of movement was astonishing; one moment he was recumbent and slothful, the next erect on his feet. The contrast between the gigantic Dawlish and the tiny page made a remarkable picture.

The page went off, and Dawlish strolled in his wake. It was not the custom of men to call at the Carilon Club and ask to see a member without giving a name. It was the habit of Patrick Dawlish to dwell upon all small and puzzling things, partly because he had a probing mind.

The waiting-room, on the ground floor, was large and as comfortable as any other room in this most respected of clubs. Its windows opened into a wide street of graceful houses. Because this was the only room where the fair sex was freely admitted, there was a concession in the shape of vases of chrysanthemums.

The solitary occupant of the room sat patiently in an arm-chair.

He was neither unknown nor mysterious to Dawlish. He was a friend, and he was a policeman. He stood up, his lips curving in a sardonic smile. He was a handsome man, and unless one were told so on good authority, one would not be likely to believe that he was Superintendent William Trivett, known to be a member of the Big Five at Scotland Yard. He looked young; in fact, he was just over forty. His hair was dark, and there was hardly a speck of grey in it. He had a close-trimmed moustache, and might have been taken for a guards' officer.

'Well, well,' said Dawlish. 'And they actually let you in.'

'The standard's been falling off here for years,' said Trivett. They shook hands.

'Sit down, Bill,' said Dawlish, and pulled up a chair for himself. 'Everyone all right?'

'Couldn't be better.'

'Crime?' asked Dawlish, as if he hoped for a less favourable answer.

'I've known it a lot worse.'

'Ah,' said Dawlish, owlishly. 'A happy policeman. Things are looking up. Well, a nearly happy policeman. No one at Scotland Yard could be really happy if he thought it worth while coming to the Carilon Club on a bleak afternoon, just to say hallo to a member. I mean, it's not Scotland Yard's dream of delight. No bad men at the Carilon Club.'

'Aren't there?' asked Trivett, lightly.

'Of course, there can't be anything in it, but how can I resist asking myself why the said highly placed policeman came. There must be a reason.'

'Oh, there's a reason,' said Trivett. 'I didn't come simply to say hallo. Busy?'

'Terribly! My dear chap, what a question! Never been so busy in my life. Had to rush up to town on urgent business. Pigs. And a curious winter blight on the Bramleys.'

'Pity,' said Trivett. 'I thought that when you'd picked all the apples and settled the big pigs and little pigs for the winter, you hibernated for the rest of the year and started poking your nose in the air again after Christmas. What are you doing in Town?'

'I've told you.'

'You're a smooth liar,' said Trivett. 'This is a serious question. Are you fiddling around on some job that we ought to be doing?'

'No,' said Dawlish simply.

'I hope you're telling the truth,' said Trivett. 'I had an interesting half-hour with the Assistant Commissioner this morning. Your name cropped up. He said it would be a good idea if we sent a couple of men to follow you, you'd been quiet so long that it was ominous. He said he wished you would either become a policeman or go and settle in Australia or South America. He said that he was tired of seeing your name in the headlines and of foolish newspapermen writing you up as a heaven-sent detective whose life's duty it was to guide Scotland Yard in the performance of its labours. He said you ought to have been locked up or murdered years ago, and you're a living proof of the theory that some creatures have nine lives. He also said . . .'

Trivett paused. He had maintained his voice at a monotonous level, as if he were giving evidence on some trifling case at the Magistrates' Court. Now, he paused as if to give emphasis to what was to follow, sat up, and touched Dawlish's arm.

'He also said that if by any freak of chance you were living the life of a law-abiding citizen, weren't mixing yourself up in some murky crime, and were not being quixotic about some sweet young thing in trouble, that it was possible you could help us. Of course, if you're busy—'

'I'm busy on my lawful occasions. The pressure of work would bow the shoulders of Atlas. Why, I seldom get more than nine hours' sleep a night and one in the afternoon. Also, I'm married. You ought to get to know my wife, one day.'

'I know that Felicity—'

'You obviously do *not* know Felicity,' said Dawlish firmly. 'Otherwise you wouldn't pass on ridiculous messages from absurd Assistant Commissioners. My wife is opposed to cooperation with the lower strata of society, like Scotland Yard men and such-like.'

Trivett chuckled.

'Well, what about it?' he asked. 'Here's a semi-official request from Scotland Yard, we think you could lend a useful hand.'

'I doubt it. In fact, I'm already harbouring dark suspicions about you, your Assistant Commissioner, and your motives. I mean, you might know that a whirlwind is blowing up and it's a job I'd love to have a sniff at. So you may be planting a little bit of nonsense on me, in the fond hope that you're going to keep my nose out of the big stuff.'

'Oh, nothing like that,' said Trivett, and looked so surprised that Dawlish was half-convinced. 'I don't know that this will be very big. It might be. We're after a man who might be law-abiding, and who might be one of the nastiest pieces of work we've seen for a long time. You could get to know him much easier than we.'

'Oh? How?'

'Just a social acquaintance, for a start. If we tackle him ourselves it would have to be official, and we don't want him warned yet. It's one of the oldest games in the world—or that's what it looks like. Pretty girls disappear. Just as simple as that.'

Dawlish looked solemn.

'My wife would love me to spend the next few weeks chasing sweet young things.'

'She wouldn't object to this. It would be a relief for her to know you had official approval, she would know you couldn't run your head against a brick wall while you were doing this.'

'I shall leave the decision to Felicity,' said Dawlish firmly. 'Last time I ventured in the narrow lanes of adventure, as one might say, we both came within minutes of being murdered. Felicity didn't enjoy it. Mind you, before I even put it to Fel, I'll need to know that it's something I might be able to tackle. That leads to the greatest problem—why come to me here?'

'The man we're interested in is a member of the Carilon Club,' said Trivett.

CHAPTER TWO

SUSPECT MEMBER

There was a hush in the room, hardly disturbed by the traffic noises outside. Upon Dawlish's face had settled an expression of horror, only partly affected.

'Impossible,' mumbled Dawlish. 'Carilon Club members don't do away with pretty girls.'

'A Carilon Club member could turn out to be bad as well as a member of a billiards club in the Mile End Road. Pat, we need help with this case, and we think this chap may be involved. You could probably find out much more easily than we can. There are several things we'd like you to do—there'll be ways for you that are almost impossible for us.'

'Nice to hear,' mumbled Dawlish. 'Spying isn't my line. I mean, fellow member and all that kind of thing. If I were persuaded that he might be a nasty piece of work I don't think scruples would stand in my way. But your tactics—oh, William! Why come here? Why tell Samuel Vye that you want to consult me? He may be the soul of discretion, but he'll be bound to tell someone who'll pass it on, and the chances of it reaching the suspect member are about fifty-fifty. Reckless waste of opportunities, William.'

Trivett coloured.

'The member concerned isn't here.'

'I should hope not. But he'll come back. And if he's what you think he is, he'll have a pretty clear idea what you'll do—ask me to co-operate. He will be so sure of that, that any approach I made would reek of suspicion. Even if you'd telephoned me and we'd met in a dark corner, he'd know that there was danger lurking in the Carilon Club. I mean, the newspapers have splashed me and the fact that we work together and all that kind of thing. Bill—I don't think you and the Assistant Commissioner have really thought about this.'

'Haven't we?' asked Trivett, almost nastily.

'Oh, well,' said Dawlish. 'I'll have a chat with Felicity. Who's the suspect member?'

'I'll tell you if you decide to play.'

'I shall catch an early evening train home and be at Haslemere in time for dinner. Unless Felicity has some pressing subject for discussion, we'll get around to this about half-past ten. By midnight she will probably be so tired of saying no that she'll say yes. How many pretty girls, so far?'

'Five.'

'Famous or infamous?'

'Nice, middle-class girls.'

'Ambitious?'

'I don't follow.'

'I mean, stage and all that kind of thing.'

'One was on the stage—just on, she'd only been out of a training school for a couple of months. The others weren't anything in particular—just nice middle-class girls, the only thing they appear to have in common is their looks. Oh—and they either knew or met the suspect member.'

'Well, well,' said Dawlish. 'I'm nearly convinced. He smiled amiably, and stood up. 'I'll telephone you from Haslemere in the morning. Don't be too surprised if an irate female comes tearing into your office first, waving an axe or an umbrella, to belabour or behead you for trying to tear me away from the piggery.'

They went together towards the door.

'Don't get this wrong,' Trivett said. 'It's serious.'

Trivett went out into the shadowy light of the November afternoon.

Wisps of fog hung in the air, it might become thick and unpleasant before the day was out. Dawlish stood and watched the detective out of sight and stared into the street, as if the fog were already so thick that he couldn't see through it. Gradually, his wooden expression changed and he turned and went into the club, his lips curved with a smile.

Ex-Sergeant-Major Samuel Vye, the chief porter, saluted him.

'Going back to-night, sir?'

'Oh, yes. That's the trouble with us country members, isn't it? Birds of passage, Sam.'

'Sir?'

'You know Mr. Trivett, of course. You've heard ridiculous stories about my own silly pranks while pretending to be a detective!'

Samuel Vye smiled broadly and understandingly.

'There have been times when people have called here to make inquiries about me,' went on Dawlish dreamily. 'Nasty pieces of work, most of them, although they've looked all right from the outside. It could happen again.'

'If it does, sir, I'll tell you.'

'Yes, good. Thanks.' Dawlish winked. 'This is a conspiracy, and you are in it. If some cove blows in and wants to know who Trivett came to see or whether I've seen Trivett, you may tell him.'

'*Tell* him, sir?'

'Oh, yes. Deceiving the enemy by appearing to let him think we are unsuspicious, Sam. You will also tell me, of course, and find out everything you can about him. Don't be surprised if it's someone you wouldn't suspect of wanting to know. In fact, don't be surprised at anything. Oh—and don't let anyone else know that Trivett and I had a little chat. If you do, then you might give the information away and I wouldn't be told about it. Just you and me together, Sam.'

'Understood, sir. Yes, sir.'

'Very good, Sergeant-Major!'

Dawlish winked, Samuel Vye beamed, and Dawlish sauntered back towards the smoking-room, but did not go all the way. There were telephone booths near it. He entered one and dialled a number. After a long pause there was an answer in a deep, almost sepulchral voice.

'What, *awake*?' asked Dawlish, as if astounded.

'Eh? Oh. *You.*' Withering scorn sounded in the deep voice. 'I might have known. I was extremely busy. Go away.'

'Yes, Mr. Jeremy,' said Dawlish, with mock humility. 'I'm sorry, Mr. Jeremy. I was only wondering, Mr. Jeremy, if you would care to come and have tea with me and—er—some cake. *Very* nice cake. Mixed fruit, I shouldn't wonder, with some icing.'

There was a pause.

'When?'

'Now.'

'My dear chap! No. Where? The club?'

'Certainly not. Cherry's.'

'Impossible,' said Jeremy. 'Four-thirty?'

'Four-fifteen.'

'Utterly impossible,' said Jeremy. 'Good-bye.'

He rang off.

Dawlish put in four more pennies, dialled another number but received no reply. He left the booth and went to the cloakroom for his hat and raincoat. As he did so, he took out a gold cigarette-case, a present from his wife, and lit a cigarette. His friends would have judged that significant, because it was only when he was very preoccupied that he smoked cigarettes instead of a pipe. Dressed suitably for the November murk, he went out, nodding to Samuel Vye, and strolled towards Piccadilly. It was not actually raining and not actually foggy, but both rain and fog would probably come before the night was out. London fascinated him; held him in a bear hug that would never loosen. He had lived in the country for many years, had imagined that nostalgia for these greasy pavements and this roar of traffic would gradually die; it didn't.

He took to the side streets, the little alleys, the unexpected turnings. He passed through tiny 'villages' of shops which looked dilapidated, and as if they belonged to the outskirts of some country town, with their scantily dressed windows and fourth-rate cafés. He walked over cobbles, went through a mews where stables had been turned into garages and yet still looked like stables.

At the end of one of these, he turned into Cherry's.

The entrance was narrow, there was a small window with a single oil-painting on a small easel against a background of dark-blue velvet. As a side-line, Cherry's sold oil-paintings; no one ever knew why. It was owned by two middle aged spinsters, the Misses Drew to those who knew their place and Floss and Flo to cronies, old customers, and the *nouveau riche*. Inside, it was spacious, for two shops had been turned into one. There was comfortable room to sit down, there was restful decoration, pieces of pottery and rare china round the walls, a large inglenook fire-place. Outwardly it had nothing to do with the heart of London; entering it, one seemed to be in a country inn, where time slipped by unnoticed and nothing changed.

Dawlish had to bend his head to get inside.

A fire blazed, the lights were dim, a dozen people were chattering, cups clattering; here was London at peace in the middle of the afternoon. A waitress approached Dawlish, and it was difficult to tell one waitress from another, because they were all grey-haired, middle-aged and dressed as maids might have been dressed years ago, in frills and furbelows.

'Hallo, Maud,' said Dawlish.

'It's very nice to see you, Mr. Dawlish. Are you alone?'

Dawlish put his head on one side and spoke so that only Maud could hear.

'Yes, Maud,' he said. 'And no. I believe that a little chap followed me. He's wearing a fawn-coloured raincoat that's a little too long for him and a trilby hat that probably cost twenty-seven and sixpence at a store. It was bought last week, I'd say. Oh, and he has brown shoes that need cleaning. Of course, he might not be there. Let me go to a place where I can make sure if he is, will you?'

CHAPTER THREE

THE ROOM UPSTAIRS

'Why, yes, sir,' said Maud in a voice which carried all over the room, 'of course you can go upstairs if you'd rather, there's only the electric fire up there, but you won't mind that, will you?'

'Not a bit.'

Dawlish beamed at her and went, at his slow gait, towards the stairs at the far end of the room. At the narrow landing he turned into a smaller room, used for special occasions and special guests. This was empty now, or Maud wouldn't have sent him up here.

It had a dormer window, which overhung the street. Chintz curtains were drawn back, and there was a comfortable window-seat. He took off his hat and went to the window, but didn't sit down. He stood to one side, and it was unlikely that anyone in the street would see him in this murky dusk. He peered right, in the direction from which he had come; no one was in sight. He peered left.

Standing at a corner nearby, inspecting a parked car, was a small man with a fawn-coloured raincoat, a new grey trilby, and a pair of brown shoes.

Dawlish smiled, as if fully satisfied, went out and used a dial telephone on the landing. This time there was no quick response, and he frowned and scratched the bridge of his nose. He was about to put the receiver down when a voice sounded, breathless and, because of that, somewhat less deep than it had been half an hour ago.

'Hallo?'

'You'll be late,' reproved Dawlish.

'Pat, you fool! I was downstairs, had to come rushing back—'

'It'll get you in training, and it's nice to know you feel energetic already. I think we'll have a guest for tea. I don't know his name, but he's hanging about outside Cherry's.' Dawlish described the little man. 'If you could persuade him to come and have a cup with us, I think we might have fun.'

Jeremy sounded outraged.

'At Cherry's?'

'Oh, no rumpus. Just a little light conversation with a man who'll probably think that the cake is poisoned. Don't be long, will you? And come in the back way.'

As Dawlish put down the receiver, a middle-aged grey-haired woman, who looked a replica of Maud, came half-way up the stairs, and smiled when she saw him.

'Tea in a quarter of an hour, Bessie,' said Dawlish. 'For three. The other two will probably come in the back way, tell them about it downstairs, will you?' Dawlish winked, and went back.

He chose the window-seat again, and this time sat down without attempting to conceal himself from the man in the street. The man's interest in the parked car had waned, and he was now studying the closed door of a garage. That lasted only five minutes, however, and he strolled farther along, taking one glance up at Cherry's window. As he glanced, Dawlish stared straight in front of him and appeared to be taking no interest in the street.

His interest revealed itself again when a tall, thin man turned a corner.

This was Tim Jeremy; and Jeremy walked as if he were trying to beat the record for the London-to-Brighton road race. He wore a raincoat and a trilby, the trilby on the back of his head. The front of his hair showed, almost jet black. He had thin features; in some moods he could look almost handsome and in others positively ugly.

The little man saw but appeared not to be interested in Jeremy.

Jeremy whirled upon him. and appeared to slip. He clutched the little man's arm. His lips were close enough to the man's head for him to whisper. The little man tried to pull himself away, but failed—Jeremy's grip could be like a vice. Next moment, they disappeared along a narrow alley which led to the back of the buildings here, and also to the back of Cherry's.

Dawlish lit a cigarette, and waited hopefully.

Five minutes later, footsteps sounded on the stairs, and were followed by Jeremy's voice, cajoling and pleading; as an old maid might talk to a cat.

'Now come along, Poppy, don't hang back. . . . I won't hurt you. . . . Just come and have a nice cup of tea with me and a friend of mine. . . . If you kick me like that again I shall have to get rough. . . . Come along, now, ups-a-daisy.'

The door opened.

The little man was propelled into the room by an unseen force. But for Dawlish's outstretched arm, he would have crashed into the tea-table. Dawlish's great hand spread across his chest, and he reeled back. Jeremy, now inside, took his arm.

The door closed.

Dawlish considered the two of them, and asked:

'Why Poppy?'

'My dear chap! His eyes positively popped out of his head. He bit and scratched and struggled all the way along the alley. I had to smack him to get him down the passage and up the stairs. He doesn't seem to *want* any tea.'

'Now look here,' the little man protested in a thin, frightened voice. 'I don't know what the game is, I'll have the police on you if—'

His voice trailed off. It was Dawlish's expression which had dried the words on his lips. He had a nondescript face, round and pale, with pale-grey eyes and colourless lips. He needed a shave. Jeremy held his brand-new trilby, and he had fair, fluffy hair, with a bald patch.

Into the silence came Bessie's voice.

'Are you ready, sir?'

Jeremy pushed up a chair, and put his hands on the little man's shoulders, thrusting him on to the chair.

Poppy was still looking at Dawlish's face—and still had that scared expression. It lingered while footsteps came sturdily up the stairs. Tea-things clinked in the tray Bessie was carrying.

Bessie opened the door and came in, carrying the tray in one hand, skilful as everyone had to be at Cherry's. She beamed. She brought the tea, wafer-thin bread and butter, jam which looked as if it contained whole apricots. To this she added a plate of cakes that would obviously melt in the mouth.

'I'll bring some more hot water soon, sir.'

'Thanks, Bessie.'

The little man whose name they didn't know gave her a frightened glance, and she didn't appear to notice it. Jeremy began to pour out tea. Dawlish held out the plate of bread and butter.

'Hungry, Poppy?'

'You—you've no right—'

'My dear chap! No crime to offer you some tea, is there?'

'Sugar? Milk?' asked Jeremy.

'Look—look here, what's the game?'

'Your game,' said Dawlish. 'You were outside the Carilon Club, and followed me here. In fact, you've three questions to answer, Poppy. Who are you? Who sent you? What were your orders?'

'You're dreaming!'

'Am I?' asked Dawlish softly.

The change came over his expression again, and in it there was a quality which frightened the man much more than Jeremy's violence had.

He licked his lips and averted his eyes; he even accepted a cup of tea. He began to sip, while the others seemed to relish their tea as if this were the most pleasant little tea-party anyone could imagine.

It was ten minutes before the little man began to talk.

Precisely forty minutes later, Dawlish went to the telephone on the landing again, and dialled Whitehall 1212.

'Hallo, who's that?' Trivett sounded preoccupied.

'The unsuspected Club Member,' said Dawlish.

'What, have you made up your mind already?' Trivett chuckled.

'Do you know a man named Rumbold—Frederick Rumbold, who lives in Wonstead Street, Fulham?'

'Not offhand.'

'Pity. He was outside the club when I left and showed a great personal interest. So I gave him some tea. He's gone home now, with Tim on his heels. He says that a Mrs. Geraldine Lorne pays him five pounds a day to watch the Carilon Club. He was to report if I turned up and if Trivett or any other policeman called to see me. So I'm also wondering if you know sweet Geraldine,' said Dawlish.

'Yes, I know Mrs. Lorne,' Trivett said heavily. 'She didn't miss the club angle, then. You'd better come over and see me, you're already in this.'

'Decision to-morrow,' said Dawlish firmly. 'Just one trifling question. Do you expect violence?'

'Not necessarily.' Trivett sounded as if he were trying to choose his words with especial care. 'There has been violence in another case which might be connected with this, but the connection isn't proved. Mrs. Lorne and the club member haven't used violence, as far as we know. Why?'

'I should hate Tim to run into a packet,' said Dawlish.

'Pat, stop fooling and come and see me. I can give you the whole story, and you'll be able to judge the odds better.'

'I will telephone you in the morning,' Dawlish said firmly. 'Keep an eye on Tim for me to-night, will you?'

He rang off.

He wiped his forehead and it was damp, although there was no reason for it. He couldn't understand why he felt that Tim, who had gone to follow Rumbold, might run into serious trouble. A hunch? Trivett and others would use the word, and scoff—and yet take notice. He was so uneasy that he telephoned the number from which he had received no answer early in the afternoon.

There was still no answer.

It was now nearly half-past five, and quite dark. He'd come up by train because his car was being overhauled, and he needed it more for running about Haslemere then he did in London. He could catch the six-fifteen, which stopped only at Woking and Guildford, and would get him home in reasonable time for dinner.

He was not sure that he ought to leave London.

He left Cherry's and walked towards Piccadilly, where he

would probably pick up a taxi for Waterloo. He wasn't followed. He had worked too often at games like this to be in doubt, although shadowing was easier by night than by day.

Even at Waterloo Station, he still wasn't satisfied that he was wise to catch the train.

It was already at the platform. He bought three evening papers, looked for a first-class carriage, and found only one empty seat. Pity—if there'd been none, he could have regarded that as an omen. In the distance, the station loudspeaker blared a message; the words were inaudible here. The whistle sounded, then a man came hurrying along the platform, and another, out of sight, said:

'Hold it, Tom, the police want to find someone. They're looking for a big chap, name of Dawlish, I think, I saw him come along the platform. First-class, I'd say. Know where he is?'

CHAPTER FOUR

TROUBLE FOR TIM

Tim Jeremy left Cherry's five minutes before Dawlish telephoned Trivett, and strolled along with an arm on the arm of Mr. Frederick Rumbold, of Fulham. Rumbold was now a pale, frightened man; frightened not only of the men who had taken him to tea, but of something else. Rumbold had talked and had reason to believe that it was dangerous to talk about his employers.

Rumbold's behaviour convinced Tim that he had told the truth. Had he lied and got away with it, he would have been much perkier.

Tim expected Rumbold to make a run for it.

Rumbold walked obediently beside him. They reached Piccadilly, and Tim said:

'Now run along, little man and don't make the mistake of annoying Patrick Dawlish again. Next time, he might get cross.'

Rumbold gave him a nervous, incredulous glance, and then slipped into a stream of people going towards the Circus. Jeremy followed. The little man didn't look round, but seemed to take it for granted that he had really been allowed to go scot free.

Jeremy let him get half a block away before he really started to walk, drew nearer in a crowd which was held up at some traffic lights, and watched him scurrying on. Wherever Rumbold was going, it wasn't Fulham; and he had said he lived at Fulham. On the other hand, he had also said that he worked for Mrs. Geraldine Lorne, who had a flat in a luxury block in Mayfair.

He passed the road which would have led to that luxury block.

Now and again Jeremy glanced behind him, but noticed no one who appeared to be following him. He kept pace with Rumbold easily, never letting the man get more than fifty yards ahead of him.

At the Circus, Rumbold slipped across Regent Street and then towards the Regent Palace Hotel and the narrow street which led to the right and towards Shaftesbury Avenue and Soho. Here the street lamps seemed to be dim, most of the shops were closed. Here and there was a lighted window, usually of a restaurant or café. Few people walked here, and most who did seemed furtive. Rumbold had turned a corner and vanished.

Jeremy reached it.

Rumbold appeared beneath a street lamp, some way along a narrow road.

Jeremy quickened his pace, because it was now possible that Rumbold realised he was being followed. The little man did not seem to be walking at any great pace, however, just trotted along, looking neither right or left. They turned two more corners and found themselves in a long, narrow street, where there were few lights; and not a single lighted window on the ground floor.

Rumbold went on.

Jeremy saw him pause, look up at a dark doorway as if checking the number, and then pass. Jeremy slowed down; the man would enter one of these places, and it would be fairly easy to see which.

Rumbold turned into a doorway.

No light shone from it.

Jeremy drew up. There was sufficient light for him to see the doorsteps. Most of the doors were closed, but here and there one stood open. Jeremy stopped at one of these, peering down. In the narrow hall beyond, there were the marks of footsteps; and this was about the spot where Rumbold had disappeared.

There was no sound.

Jeremy listened intently, made sure that he could hear nothing. He could just see the staircase. Was he wise to go on, or should he wait outside and see who else went in or came out? He had the number and name of the street, that was what Dawlish wanted most.

Jeremy grinned in the darkness, and stepped into the hallway. There was utter stillness; it was hard to believe that Rumbold had gone in here.

He went nearer the foot of the stairs.

As he reached them, he heard a creak from behind him. He turned, abruptly, and fear, naked as flame, scorched him.

A man, big and shadowy, smashed a blow at his head. The blow was powerful enough to send him reeling back. He kicked against the bottom stair and fell backwards—and he could see the shadowy figure moving forward.

Then hands brushed his throat.

He felt the pressure of long fingers, biting suddenly into his flesh, searching for his windpipe. The pressure increased, his breath was cut off. He tried to swing his arms but only hit the wall and banisters. He twisted, but the fingers gripped like steel, and the pressure was agonising. He tried to breathe, and his lungs seemed to blow up like a balloon, pain was like a red-hot band across his chest.

He felt his senses whirling.

He lost consciousness.

At Waterloo Station Dawlish stood up and reached the door as the two men who had been talking about him peered into the compartment.

'Looking for me?' he asked.

'Oh, yes, sir. You Mr. Dawlish?'

'That's right.'

'Message from Superintendent Trivett of Scotland Yard, sir,' said the porter, eyeing him with obvious respect. 'Will you please telephone him at once?'

Dawlish climbed down, and the whistles shrilled out again. The train had left the platform by the time he reached the ticket barrier. The porter escorted him to a booking-office where a telephone was put at his disposal. He asked for Scotland Yard and looked about him woodenly as he waited for the call to come through.

'Scotland Yard, can I help you?' a girl asked.

'Mr. Trivett, please. Dawlish here.'

'One moment, sir.'

One moment grew into several minutes. He began to fret; if Trivett wanted him in such a hurry, why didn't he come on the line?

'Listen, Pat,' said Trivett suddenly. 'I'm damnably sorry about this. Tim's caught a nasty packet. He's at the Westminster Hospital, and it's touch and go. A bashed head and strangulation. He was found in an empty house in Lester Street, Soho. So was Rumbold—and Rumbold was dead,' Trivett said.

Dawlish said heavily, 'I see.' Clerks were glancing at him covertly, but his expression was quite blank. 'How?'

'Strangulation.'

'Caught anyone?'

'No. Nothing helpful has turned up yet. You remember asking me about Mrs. Geraldine Lorne. One of the people we wanted you to contact was this Mrs. Lorne. She knows your club member, whose name is Kane. Call him to mind?'

There was only one man at the Carilon nearly as large as Dawlish, and his name was Sebastian Kane. Dawlish pictured a dark-haired, heavily moustached giant with a tremendous reputation for big-game hunting in South America.

'Yes,' he said.

'We know a bit about the association between him and Mrs. Lorne, and the five girls all knew her, too. We'd like you to go and see her—just as you would have done if you knew nothing about the attack on Tim and Rumbold, and without any priming from me. Just size her up, as you would if you'd started this off by yourself.'

'Why don't you go?'

'We think you can get more out of her. We'd like to get your reaction—because we think you might get another of your bright notions. You're always at your best when you're not primed with background. You seem to get a new slant, and we want one.'

'All right, I'll go. Tell Felicity I'm delayed, will you? Blame yourself for it, but don't mention Tim to her.'

He rang off, and wiped his forehead, forced himself to say 'Thanks' to the man who had let him use the telephone, and went out into the station. The crowds pushed past him, the bookstalls were thronged.

He was lucky to find a taxi at once, gave the woman's address, then sat back and lit a cigarette. His expression was bleak; he could imagine Tim, struggling for breath, fighting against death.

The taxi pulled up, outside a block of flats in Milden Street, before he realised they were anywhere near.

CHAPTER FIVE

GERALDINE

Dawlish was jolted out of his bleak reverie, by the taxi-driver's gruff:

'Here we are, Guv'nor.'

Dawlish turned to survey the pale-grey block of flats—Hailey Court. It was within a stone's throw of Grosvenor Square, not far from Park Lane and Oxford Street, as near the heart of London as anything could be. It was also quite near Cherry's. There were two main entrances, each lighted discreetly, and hinting at the luxury beyond. Outside each stood a commissionaire with a large umbrella.

The nearer one came forward, and had to stretch his arm up very high in order to cover Dawlish.

'What number, sir?'

'Thirty-one, I think. Mrs. Lorne.'

'That's right, sir, this entrance.'

Inside, a smaller but equally splendid commissionaire took care of him, informed him that Mrs. Lorne was in, and took him to the third floor in a lift which would have been suitable in a royal palace.

Dawlish approached this door along a wide, carpeted passage. The carpet was of a light-brown colour, the walls appeared to be made of beaten gold, fresh flowers decorated small alcoves. At intervals there were larger alcoves, and one of these was just beyond the door of Number 31. It was large enough to hide Dawlish.

The lift whined, very softly, and gates clanged mutedly at the next floor. Dawlish remained hidden. Another muted clang told him that the lift had started to go down, and it whirred again. Still Dawlish hid. He stood close to the wall, ears strained to catch any sound, and fancied he heard a footfall. He did not look round. The footfall was repeated, and he was quite sure that a man was approaching. Next, he heard the sound of breathing. He faced the passage, as a hand swung into view, and then a man appeared.

The man's mouth rounded in an O of astonishment when he saw Dawlish.

'Good evening,' said Dawlish, and stretched out his hands. He curved his fingers round the man's throat and squeezed-gently, although he knew that this was how Tim had been attacked. The eyes of the man in his grip rivalled poor Poppy Rumbold's.

Dawlish eased the pressure.

'Looking for me? You were downstairs, watching, and when you saw me arrive, you followed,' said Dawlish in a conversational voice. 'You went up to the next floor, to make sure that I shouldn't notice you, and didn't come into sight until you'd made sure that I wasn't outside Madame's door. Right?'

The man nodded, as vigorously as he dare; and anyone looking into Dawlish's face might have been forgiven if he'd expected to be murdered.

'Confession's still good for the soul, this might reform you,' said Dawlish, and let him go. He swayed back, clutching at his throat and thus sticking his chin out. Dawlish clipped him beneath the chin, his teeth clicked together and his eyes rolled.

Dawlish stopped him from falling.

He lifted him, carried him a little way along to the next and last alcove, where there was a sizeable couch. He laid him behind the couch, used his tie to bind his wrists, and then investigated his means of trousers support; the man used both belt and braces. Dawlish took the belt off and bound his victim's ankles, then used a handkerchief as a gag. He straightened up, pushed the man still nearer the wall and stood the couch in front of him.

Anyone passing could see him; but there was a reasonable chance that no one would pass in the next half-hour or so.

Dawlish went back to the door of Number 31, and pressed a bell which was set in a gilded lily flower; it was not surprising that the builders of this magnificence had even tried to gild the lily.

Footsteps sounded at once, and then a girl opened it. She was small and nicely built, had big grey eyes and a pleasant smile; she could be called beautiful. She seemed tiny against the massive height of Dawlish, and she had to crane her head to look up into his face. Yet his size hadn't startled her.

'Good afternoon. Is Mrs. Lorne in? I'm Patrick Dawlish.'

'Please come in.'

She stood aside, and Dawlish stepped into a square hall. Here the gilt had changed to silver, there were many mirrors, the carpet made the one outside seem threadbare. This was a large apartment, with a passage off which several doors led, and the hall also had three rooms leading off it.

She led the way to a door which was partly open, thrust it wider, and stepped aside again. Her smile was the smile of an angel. She had wavy brown hair, soft and rather fluffy. She wore a simply cut dress of green material, had nice hands, and remarkably nice legs.

Dawlish stepped into the room.

It was empty.

'I won't keep you a moment,' the girl said, and disappeared.

She did not close the door.

Dawlish looked round, and marvelled that anyone should revel in quite such luxury as this. The powder blue of carpet and furnishings had a soft restfulness. The furniture was silvery coloured—including the grand piano, which stood in one corner. There were no pictures on the walls, only masks of young women; pretty young women, too, and they were beautifully made—they looked almost real.

He stood by a fire-place which was filled with a silvered electric fire.

He listened intently, but heard no sound of a door closing, or of voices. That suggested stealth. The girl had not been surprised to see him; that suggested that she had been forewarned.

There was a movement outside, and the girl came in again. She moved well. Now that he could see her more clearly, and was less interested in seeing other things about the flat, he could admire her more dispassionately. He had not done justice to her when he had said she was nicely built; she was beautifully built.

Five pretty girls from nice middle-class families had disappeared, and Mrs. Geraldine Lorne was suspected of knowing something about that. This girl might well be Number 6.

'Well, Mr. Dawlish,' she said. 'How can I help you?' It was one of those moments when his wife's faith in his acting ability would have been rudely shaken. He was surprised and showed it; he felt as he might when discovering that he had been the victim of a confidence trick.

She smiled at him delightedly, as if she were able to share the joke.

'Yes. I'm Mrs. Lorne. Geraldine Lorne.'

She sat in a large arm-chair, which dwarfed her, and looked sweet, wholesome, and quite astoundingly attractive. Dawlish sat in an equally large arm-chair, which just held him. Not once had the smile faded from her eyes, yet he felt that it was forced—that she was not so natural as she appeared to be.

'Well, how *can* I help you, Mr. Dawlish?'

'As a matter of fact,' said Dawlish, now fully recovered and very wary, 'I think I can help you.'

'How delightful!'

'Yes, isn't it? Mr. Rumbold told me.'

'Rumbold?'

'Don't you know Freddie Rumbold?'

'I don't recall the name, but I meet so many people that it's hard to be sure. I know a lot of Freddies, but never seem to get their second names.'

'Well, what a pity,' said Dawlish. 'Freddie was so sure that you would know him.'

'What did he say?'

'He said you were mixing with bad company,' said Dawlish firmly. 'In fact, he asked me if I would try to prove to you how bad it was.'

'He must have been pulling your leg,' said Geraldine Lorne, looking as if she knew all about the joke and was in fact a party to it. 'I've hosts of friends, but I'm sure they're all most respectable. Did he mention anyone by name?'

'Yes—Sebastian Kane.'

That was intended to serve as a body blow which would shake her badly. He was showing his hand, and she wouldn't expect that. By rights she should have looked startled, then covered up her confusion, then said earnestly that she was quite sure that Dawlish was the victim of a hoax. She did none of these things. There was a moment's pause—then she threw back her lovely head and laughed, setting the fluffy hair dancing, opening her mouth and showing beautifully white teeth, even allowing him to see the tip of her tongue.

Dawlish sat poker-faced.

She stopped laughing, at last; and he was almost sorry, for laughter could be a joyous sound, and hers certainly was.

'If you knew Sebastian, you'd know how ridiculous that is,' she said. 'I wish he were here, he'd love it. Bad company! Why, he's a darling.' Her eyes were brimming over with merriment. 'In fact, he's rather like you.'

The telephone bell rang.

CHAPTER SIX

WAITING TIME

'I'm so sorry,' said Geraldine Lorne, and pressed his knee as she stood up. The telephone was just behind him. She lifted the receiver and rested her right hand on the back of his chair, just touching his shoulder. He didn't need to look round, for he could see her head and shoulders in a mirror near the piano, and her profile in another mirror opposite the door.

'Hallo, who's that?'

A sound came from the telephone, as of a deep masculine voice.

'Hallo, *dar*ling!' cried Geraldine Lorne. 'I'm so glad you've called.' She chuckled, infectiously. 'Darling, you couldn't come round, could you?'

It was just a little too bright to be true.

'But sweet, the most wonderful thing's happened,' said Geraldine. 'I've had a visitor who thinks you're a bad man— and from the way he looked at me, he thinks I'm a bad woman. . . . His name's Dawlish, and he's huge, nearly as big as you are. . . . No, darling, of course I won't. . . . Could you? . . . Half an hour, I'm sure he'll wait. 'Bye-bye!'

She put the receiver back and turned and pressed Dawlish's shoulder.

'That was Sebastian, he'll be here in half an hour. You can wait, can't you?'

'I think I could bear to.'

'Splendid! Let me get you a drink.'

She brushed her hand against his cheek as she moved, and he didn't think that was by accident. She whirled across to the cocktail cabinet. Her dress was rather short, and flared, she had the shapeliest legs a woman could have, but the more he saw of her, the tinier she appeared to be.

She poured out, expertly—and he made sure that she used the same bottles for both drinks.

She put the glass down by his side and sat on the pouf.

'You're going to love meeting Sebastian Kane,' she said.

She might mean exactly what she seemed to mean; but there could be much more than that behind her manner. In the lightest, most casual way, she had told Kane that he was here, that he suspected them of—crime.

'I don't know whether to ask you to tell me more about it, or whether to wait for Sebastian,' she said. 'Perhaps we'd better forget it until he arrives. He'll be prompt—he hates unpunctuality.'

'May I use the telephone?'

'Why, of course.' She jumped up to show him where it was, quite unnecessarily, then went across the room like a brisk wind, to the door. 'I'll be back in a minute.'

Dawlish dialled the number of the Westminster Hospital, and felt deflated. He wanted to inquire about Tim; he had also wanted the girl to hear, for she might be impressed by the slant he could give that conversation. As if she had sensed that, she had done the 'proper' thing and left him on his own. He stared at the door. He hadn't heard her cross the hall, and she might be waiting outside the door. He glanced round the room, at the mirrors; there was one against the wall above the cocktail cabinet, and he could see the reflection of the open door in that; nothing else. He kept it in sight as the ringing sound stopped.

'Westminster Hospital, can I help you?'

'I'd like to speak to the Duty Sister, please.'

'Will you hold on?'

Dawlish continued to watch the door, and then he smiled faintly; for Geraldine Lorne was there. He could see the top of her head and one of her hands reflected in the mirror.

A woman spoke.

'This is the Night Sister.'

'I am a friend of Mr. Jeremy's, who was brought in some time ago, severely injured,' Dawlish said. 'He had been strangled and battered about the head. Can you give me any news of him, please.'

'Yes,' said the Night Sister promptly. 'He is still unconscious, but there has been no change for the worse.'

'That's fine,' said Dawlish softly. 'Thank you.' He covered the mouthpiece with his hand, and spoke more loudly, 'So it's really touch and go, and you don't think he has much chance.'

The Night Sister, hearing nothing of this, said, 'Good-bye.'

Dawlish took his hand away.

'Good-bye, and thanks.'

He put the receiver down and stared in front of him. He didn't look into the mirror again. A moment later she came in brightly.

'Finished?'

'Yes, thanks.'

'I do hope nothing will delay Sebastian,' said Geraldine, as if her confidence in his punctuality had received a setback. 'I should hate you to miss him.' She went to her chair and dropped into it; her eyes were enormous, a clear and lovely grey. 'So you are *the* Mr. Dawlish? *Patrick* Dawlish? Of course I've read a lot about you. I love the scandal sheets, and they give such a lot of space to crime and sensations, you're always in the middle of some sensation, aren't you? I thought when you came in that I'd seen you before somewhere, but it must have been your photograph, that's been splashed all over the front pages, hasn't it? What *makes* a public hero?'

'Don't ask me! Can't be responsible for what the newspapers get up to.'

'Oh, modesty,' she said, and waved a hand. 'It's false modesty really, you know—Sebastian's just the same. How well do you know him?'

'Big game. Explorer. Land of the Incas, Matto Grosso, all that kind of thing. Didn't he find a new civilisation in the middle of South America, or something like that? Oh, yes, it was swallowed up by an earthquake, and only he and two of his bearers managed to escape alive.'

'That's right—it happened two years ago. He pretends he was frightened!' She laughed. 'It's a waste of time trying to convince me, and I wouldn't believe that anything could ever frighten you, either. It's funny, but you *are* alike. Have you ever been to South America?'

She was still talking when a bell rang inside the flat. She sprang up.

'That'll be Sebastian, he always forgets his key. Exactly half an hour!'

She hurried towards the door.

'Are you here alone?' asked Dawlish.

'Yes, it's such a nuisance, I have a man and a woman usually, but the woman stole and the man drank, I got so tired of it that I sent them packing this morning. I can get daily help easily of course, but you never know who you can trust these days, do you?'

The bell rang again.

'And I've a new secretary coming the day after tomorrow,' she said, and hurried away.

Dawlish heard the door open, then heard a gasp.

That came so unexpectedly that it caught him off his guard. He heard a second gasp as he sprang to his feet. There was a scuffle. He reached the door in three long strides but didn't go outside, just peered around.

He saw a man—a man of medium height wearing a trilby hat and with a scarf over his mouth and chin and the lower part of his nose. Only his eyes and cheek-bones showed clearly. He was gripping the girl's arms, and she stood with her back towards him, a white sack or a pillowcase over her head, drooping to her shoulders. He was holding her with some force, and a muffled gasp came from inside the bag.

The man had some string in his pocket and made a swift job of fastening her wrists together. Then he lifted her bodily and moved towards another door. He seemed to know the lay-out of the flat very well.

Dawlish stepped into the hall and followed the man. A light went on. The attacker would have no difficulty in holding Geraldine Lorne with one arm, while he switched on the light. Dawlish reached that doorway, found that it was the kitchen, and saw the intruder standing by the open door of the larder. He dropped the girl in heavily, then stood up and closed the door. He turned the key as Dawlish reached him, without a sound. He didn't seem to dream that Dawlish or anyone else was there, just turned—and fear leapt into beady eyes.

The man backed away, darting his right hand towards his pocket. That was a mistake. Dawlish hit him on the side of the head, an open-handed buffet which knocked the man against the larder door with a loud bang. Dawlish slid his fingers into the pocket, and drew out a gun.

He looked at it with an air of surprise, as if he didn't know what on earth it was. The man still leaned against the door. Dawlish stretched out his free hand and pulled the scarf down. It fell round the man's neck. Then he tipped the brim of the trilby back so far that the hat fell on to the floor behind the man.

He had a thin face, thin lips, and a pointed chin. His nose curved inwards, and seemed to have no bridge. He certainly had neither good looks nor a nice expression to recommend him. He stood with his mouth partly open, the left side of his face flushed, and the fear still lingering in his eyes.

'And who are you?' asked Dawlish.

'I—I work here, I left something behind, I—'

'And that's why you put Mrs. Lorne in the larder,' said Dawlish.

The reply had shaken him; nothing would go according to expectations. It was possible that this was the man who'd been dismissed at a moment's notice this morning.

Then Dawlish heard a sound behind him, stepped to one side, saw the door swinging back. It crashed into the wall, and the enormous figure of Sebastian Kane stood there, glowering, aggressive.

'What the hell's all this?' he demanded. 'Parker! What are you—'

Parker swung round, pulled open the door behind him, and as both Dawlish and Kane rushed forward, disappeared. Dawlish might have brushed a lesser man aside; there was no such case in handling Kane. They collided; it was like two tanks meeting. They swayed away from each other, while footsteps clattered down the iron fire-escape at the back of the flats.

CHAPTER SEVEN

SEBASTIAN KANE

Dawlish recovered from the collision first. He rubbed his right shoulder gently, watched Kane straighten up from the kitchen-table, which he'd pushed half-way across the room as he had fallen against it, and saw the angry glare in Kane's light-brown eyes.

'Mrs. Lorne had burglars. Or more accurately a burglar!'

'Parker? He—Where's Geraldine?'

'In the larder.'

'What the hell!' roared Kane. 'Listen, don't try to make a monkey out of me, Dawlish. You can throw your weight about with some people, but not with me.'

'So I've found. It doesn't alter the fact that she's in the larder. Parker dumped her there.'

Kane strode to the larder, and looked as if he would smash the panels with his mighty fist. He fumbled with the key, cursed, turned it, and opened the door.

'Gerry!' he cried.

Dawlish stepped past him as he bent down to pick up the girl, and went on to the top of the fire-escape. There was no sign or sound of Parker, now; it would have been a waste of time chasing after the man, who'd had too good a start. There was a wide courtyard at the back, and two passages leading from it, each lit by a wall-lamp.

Dawlish turned round.

Kane was holding the girl in his arms, cradling her as if she were a baby. He had already untied the string, so her arms were free. Now he was pulling off the white bag, gently, and he stared down at her with an expression which was almost maternal; and had a touch of fear in it. The gentleness of his movements might have surprised Dawlish, had he not known a little about Sebastian Kane.

The bag came off. Kane flung it across the room.

'My pet, are you all right? Did he hurt you? Don't talk, just keep quiet.'

He strode out of the room, and Dawlish watched him, frowning slightly, not quite sure what to make of all this. He followed, and was in time to see Kane lowering the girl to the settee, with the same gentleness. He punched a cushion and placed it over her knees, and then crouched down beside her, clutching one hand in his great paw.

'Now, tell me all about it, pet.'

Dawlish went across and poured out a gin and Italian.

'There—there isn't much to tell,' said Geraldine in a scared voice. 'There was a ring at the door, and I thought you'd left your key behind, and went to open it. A man stood there, with a scarf over his face, he hit me, and then dropped a bag over my face, I couldn't breathe. I hardly know what happened after that. Where—' She struggled up. 'Where's Dawlish?'

'Drink this, and you'll feel a new woman,' Dawlish said, revealing himself.

She sank back on the cushion.

'Thank goodness *you're* all right.'

'It wouldn't matter a damn if he weren't all right,' growled Kane. 'He ought to be shot, for allowing it to happen. Where the heck he gets his reputation from, I don't know. He let Parker get away, too.'

'Parker!'

'Yes, the swine. I told you he ought to have been flung out on his ear a long time ago. He came to steal what he could, just to get his own back. Why the blazes did you let him go, Dawlish?'

'I thought you had something to do with that.'

'Well, I didn't.'

'Sorry,' murmured Dawlish. 'Just blame me. But there won't be any difficulty in picking Parker up, if you're sure it was—'

'Sure? Are you calling me a liar?'

Kane straightened up, glaring into Dawlish's face.

He was known at the club as a man of uncertain temper, and was not very popular, either among the staff or the members; but he was respected, because of his known physical courage and the sensational things that he had done; he was regarded at the Carilon as a kind of tame gorilla; a proud possession, but one who had to be kept at a distance.

'Oh, Seb,' sighed Geraldine Lorne in a weak voice, 'I can't stand any more excitement, I really can't. *Please* be quiet.'

Kane glared.

'Hear that, Dawlish? Be quiet!' He turned and sank down on the settee, pushing the girl's legs to one side to make room. 'Now, pet, you ought to go to bed. You've had a rough time. I think a sedative—maybe you ought to have a doctor, honey.'

'No, Seb, thank you.' She smiled up at him tremulously. 'I would like a cup of tea. Think you can make one?'

Her smile would have melted the wrath of a dictator. Kane patted her shoulder, said, 'All right, honey,' straightened up, glowered at Dawlish, and strode out. He closed no doors; it sounded as if he were flinging the kettle about the kitchen, and at any moment Dawlish expected to hear the sound of breaking crockery.

Geraldine smiled at him, a little timorously.

'I'm terribly sorry,' she said. 'I was looking forward to you and Sebastian meeting so much. Now he's in this mood, I don't think there's any point in your staying. Usually he'd see the funny side of being taken for a bad man, but nothing will seem funny to him to-night, now. I know—these moods last, when they come. *Could* you make some excuse to go? Say you're going to see the police about Parker, or something. I suppose it *was* Parker.'

'You could telephone the police,' Dawlish said.

'Yes, but that wouldn't get you away. Sebastian will believe you if you say it would be better to have a word with the police yourself. And then he'll cool down, and you can see him tomorrow, if you think it's worth while. There's just one thing—you needn't worry about the bad company I'm supposed to mix with. Sebastian will look after that!' Her eyes smiled, although most of her gaiety had gone. 'Will you please go?'

'Must I?' said Dawlish.

'Well, you'll have asked for trouble,' said Geraldine. Obviously she had known her appeal was a forlorn hope. 'If you must stay, don't talk to him for a while, just let him settle down. Quiet, here he comes.'

Kane approached; it was as if an elephant were bringing the tea-tray. He put the tray on a nearby table, and there was one cup, milk, and sugar.

'Let it brew a minute,' he said. 'Now, Dawlish—'

'Darling, don't you think we ought to do something about Parker?' asked Geraldine hastily. 'Tell the police, I mean. We don't know where he lives, but the police are more likely to catch him if we tell them quickly. It would be a mistake to let him go scot free, wouldn't it?'

'The next time I see Parker,' announced Kane, 'I'll break his neck.'

'I should think he'll get a long prison sentence, if you'll act quickly,' said Geraldine.

Kane drew himself up to his full height, looked at Dawlish contemptuously, and spoke with stinging sarcasm.

'What's the great Dawlish doing? This hero who's supposed to be better than the police at their own job? There's the telephone. Report it. You let Parker get away once, want him to dodge the police, too?'

Dawlish smiled, very amiably, and there was a gleam in his eyes which would have made his wife cry out, in warning, that he oughtn't to be trusted. His voice was so gentle that it was almost a lullaby.

'Why on earth they let an ill-mannered lout like you stay in the Carilon Club, I just don't know. I shall try to do something about it. In any case, Sebastian, it's an adult club. There's no room for schoolboys.'

Kane said in a strangled voice, 'All right, you've asked for it.' He lowered his hands, with the fists clenched, and came forward rather like a gorilla—but a handsome gorilla—as if ready for mortal combat. 'Apologise,' he said.

'Mr. Dawlish, you didn't mean—'

'Every word,' said Dawlish.

Kane didn't speak; just launched himself forward, and he came like a rocket.

He leapt into a straight left which had most of Dawlish's weight behind it, and was aimed for his *solar plexus*. He knew no more about defence than a child of three, and left himself wide open; and as Dawlish had seen, he was inclined to be putting on weight, so was short in the wind. Dawlish's fist sank into his stomach. Wind hissed out of his mouth, he stood still for a split second and then his knees began to give way. He turned colour in front of Dawlish's eyes, his mouth opened and stayed open. His right hand went to his stomach, as if to make sure that it was still there, and his left groped out for support. It met the air. He went down on his knees, and began to make little groaning noises, of sheer pain.

Dawlish stepped across, went behind him, hoisted him by the shoulders, and dragged him across to a chair. He helped him into it, then gripped the back of his neck and pushed his head between his knees.

'Just stay like that, and you'll feel better soon,' he said.

He left him, and saw that Geraldine Lorne's eyes held an expression of mingled incredulity and horror.

'You—you must be mad,' she said. 'To do that to him, why, he—'

'He'll really get hurt if he leads off like that too often,' said Dawlish. 'Don't worry about me, Geraldine, I can take care of myself in spite of all the Kanes in London.'

He took her hand; it was the first time he'd touched her voluntarily. He gripped gently at first, and then more tightly—not hurtfully, but sufficient to show that if he squeezed any more, it would hurt. He looked straight into her eyes, and his expression was exactly what it had been when he had scared the wits out of Rumbold.

Dawlish said softly, 'Listen, Geraldine. Rumbold was murdered this evening, and a friend of mine was badly hurt.

You know how badly. I came here to get the truth out of you, and I'm still here, just for that. Why did you tell Rumbold to watch me at the Carilon Club? Don't lie, my pet, don't think your airs and graces will help you over this, I'm serious.'

CHAPTER EIGHT

DENIAL

She said, 'It's not true. It's just not true.'

The words were whispered, and he could only just hear them. Her expression didn't alter. She stared straight into his eyes, as if she were willing him to believe her.

'It's just not true,' she repeated. 'I swear it. I've never heard of anyone named Rumbold. Never.'

He released her hands.

Kane grunted, a less tortured sound, and the spring of the chair creaked. Dawlish looked round and saw the other giant getting up, with some difficulty. Kane's cheeks were greyish-green, and his eyes were bloodshot. He pressed one hand against his stomach, and there was neither rage nor fight left in him; although they would probably be easily re-kindled.

'Please go now,' Geraldine whispered.

Dawlish turned away and went out. The key was on the outside of the drawing-room door. He closed the door and turned the key softly, and he did not think that either of them had heard it. He waited for a few seconds, then he went into the other rooms of the flat.

There were five. A dining-room, quite small and touched with the same luxury as the drawing-room; three bedrooms, all beautifully appointed; and a small study, obviously a woman's room. Beautifully bound volumes were in open shelves, from classics to the modern poets, there were masterpieces on all the arts, and there were some modern novels.

He looked through the drawers of a small desk, made of sycamore, delightfully grained and polished. He found nothing which appeared to connect the girl with the five missing lovelies or with Rumbold. He found an address-book with a few names and addresses in it. That might come in useful; he slipped it into his pocket, and rummaged for anything to point to Rumbold and crime; and found nothing at all. He did find some correspondence with a Miss Hilda Green, who was due to take up duties as a secretary the day after to-morrow. The girl's name was in the address book.

He finished with the desk, and looked for a safe. He found a combination wall-safe behind a water-colour in the wall near the desk.

Did she keep the number in her head? Or was there a note of it?

He went back to the desk, glanced through note-books and diaries, and at the end of one small diary, which had only a list of appointments, found three different sequences of numbers, pencilled in faintly. There had been other sequences, and they had been rubbed out. He took the book to the safe and turned the knob, listening for the clicks; the first sequence had no effect; the second had none. He tried the third, and found himself hoping desperately that this would do the trick.

It did; when he pulled, the door opened.

Inside was jewellery, some one-pound notes, a few oddments of gold and silver, and one bundle of papers—share certificates; that was all.

He closed the safe and went into the main bedroom. Geraldine's handbag was on the dressing-table. He looked inside, and found several yale keys. He tip-toed to the front door, and tried them; two turned the lock. He put one into his pocket and replaced the others, took the handbag back and went along to the drawing-room.

He unlocked the door, hearing a whisper of conversation inside, but nothing else. He left the flat, closing the hall door quietly behind him. Then he walked along to the alcove where he had left the man who had followed him—and who he had assumed had been working for Geraldine Lorne.

The man wasn't there.

Dawlish rubbed the bridge of his nose, thoughtfully, and marvelled at the mysterious incidents at Hailey Court. It seemed possible to get away with anything here; men roamed at will. That might be worth thinking about, later. He went downstairs, and the two commissionaires were genial, smiling, and helpful; one went hurrying for a taxi, leaving his huge umbrella behind, although it was now raining much harder than when Dawlish had arrived. He appeared to be able to whistle taxis out of the air. Dawlish tipped, thanked, and sat back, stretching out his legs as far as they could go.

'Where to, sir?' asked the commissionaire.

'Westminster Hospital.'

A few minutes' drive away from Hailey Court, Dawlish tapped on the window.

'Make that Scotland Yard, will you?'

Trivett might not be at the Yard, but after to-night's events was more likely to be there than at his Victoria flat.

Trivett's office was on the third floor, and there was a light beneath the door. Dawlish didn't tap, just opened the door and stepped inside. Bright light shone from three lamps, on to two desks, the plain walls, the uncurtained windows—and Trivett. Trivett sat at the larger of the desks, and appeared to be surrounded by papers; the desk was untidy, and that was seldom the case with Trivett's.

'It's nice to know you do something to help earn your keep,' Dawlish said. 'Mind if I sit down?'

'Hallo, Pat. I thought you might turn up. I've just had word from the hospital by the way—Tim's in the land of the living. Complications caused by the wound in the head are causing most worry at the moment.'

'Conscious?'

'No.'

'I'd like to see him as soon as he is.'

'Does that mean you're staying in London?'

'I'm not sure. Felicity will be worried, and I could get home and be back first thing in the morning. I'll see. Anything turned up about Rumbold or Tim?'

Trivett said, 'Nothing, Pat. The house was empty. It was badly damaged a few years ago, and hasn't been let to anyone since. The ground floor was being used, without the owner's authority, but none of the prints we picked up are on our records. There was an old mattress on the floor and a couple of chairs, the remains of some food. We're questioning everyone in the district, but haven't had any results yet. As far as we can make out, Rumbold went in first, and Tim followed him. Tim was found at the foot of the stairs, Rumbold in the room. A man with powerful fingers did the strangling—nothing else was used.'

'Who found them?'

'One of our men—the front door was open, he shone his light inside and saw Tim.'

Trivett paused, pushed cigarettes across the desk, waited until Dawlish had lit up, and then asked:

'Did you see Mrs. Lorne?'

'Yes. Know her?'

'Only by sight.'

'You should have warned me,' Dawlish said. 'When I first saw her I thought she was one of her own victims. If she has any victims. Bill, I don't think anything about Geraldine Lorne or Sebastian Kane is going according to your fond hopes.'

'So she won you over. That's one reason why I wanted you to see her without any background story.' There was a hard note in his voice. 'Now you've seen her, you can know what I know. She's promiscuous, wanton—'

He broke off.

'As bad as that?'

'If her reputation doesn't lie, yes. She married an old man, four years ago. He was an Australian here on holiday. They spent most of their time in the South of France, came here for a month a year after they were married—and he died. She thought he would leave her the better part of a million pounds, but actually he left only a few thousand. She's done well for herself, since.

'She went back to France, but kept a country cottage in England. Most of what I know is second-hand—from the French police and from the police at St. Albans—her cottage was near there. She seems to be completely amoral; to have a way of making a man think he's the only one who matters in the world. The reports from France and St. Albans are about the same. Everything's sweet and clean on the surface, but most of the parties have been pretty foul. They've all been small, very few guests, but—I know you're thinking that the sweet and saintly Geraldine Lorne couldn't do that kind of thing. Well, there isn't much doubt. Her English efforts have been very carefully secluded, but a St. Albans inspector went to see her, six months ago. She was all hoity-toity, denied it all, but sold the house and took over this place. I didn't know anything about it until I found the connection between the missing girls and the little lady. Then I discovered a queer thing: the St. Albans man died, soon afterwards, in a hit-and-run accident.'

'Are you seriously suggesting that your St. Albans man was murdered?'

'No, I'm simply asking myself if he saw something at the house which Mrs. Lorne afterwards realised was dangerous. So far as the inquest is concerned it was manslaughter.'

'I see,' said Dawlish. 'I had a good look round and didn't find any indication of this in her library, no filthy pictures, nothing pornographic, unless the binding says one thing and the book another. I doubt it. How long has she known Kane?'

'Since she married. Her husband introduced them.'

'Nice of him.'

'Lorne was an orchid lover. He had a wonderful collection in Australia, and made another in France—it was passed on to Kew Gardens on his death. He helped to finance Kane's last expedition into the Matto Grosso, and Kane brought back some unknown specimens. Kane was away when he died.'

'Any suspicions about how Lorne died?'

'He hadn't been under a doctor in England, and died suddenly, so they opened him up. The best men we have all agreed that it was quite natural—cardiac failure and cerebral haemorrhage. Later reports from Australia said that he'd had one or two strokes some years ago, recovered temporarily, and then got one that laid him out. At the time, we didn't know anything about his wife, the *post mortem* was just routine. We still don't know much about his wife. She was only a girl when he met her, isn't much more now. No parents we can trace, only an old aunt who disowned her, not liking her ways. As for friends, the parties were always very small, half a dozen or so.'

'How long after her husband's death did Geraldine start her party tricks?'

'A few months.'

'Before or after Kane returned?'

'Oh, after,' said Trivett. 'She's had several close men friends—if anyone can be a close friend after a few weeks' acquaintance—but they've all faded out; her pace was too hot. We know a few of them, but haven't yet been justified in questioning them. We might have an excuse now.'

'Let me,' said Dawlish.

'We'll see. Kane has stayed in her favour, or else hasn't tired of her, and that may be because he's often away. There's one odd thing, Pat. Practically all Geraldine Lorne's paramours have been big men. Either big or pretty good physical specimens. She seems to worship size and manly strength. That was one reason why I thought you might have a shot at her—had you agreed to play, earlier, I'd have trotted out Geraldine's name.'

'Nice of you,' murmured Dawlish. 'Now could I be told something about the five missing lovelies?'

Trivett didn't answer at once, but stubbed out his cigarette sat back, and studied Dawlish.

At last, he said, 'Definitely your job now?'

'Yes.'

'You won't change your mind if Felicity should object?'

'No. She won't, when she knows what's happened to Tim.'

'Well, that's your pigeon,' Trivett said. 'These girls—I've a list of their names and addresses here, everything you'll need to work on—were all ex-secretaries to Geraldine Lorne—even the little actress one, who started life as a shorthand-typist. None lasted more than a month. According to the parents, they all said they couldn't stand the type of life she led and expected them to lead. The parties and whatnot. She was always charming with them, paid them well, gave them full expenses, and a month's money when they left. They were employed over a period of fifteen months, but none of them worked at Hailey Court, she hasn't had a secretary since she went to live there. They all knew Sebastian Kane, who was always in and out of the cottage and the French villa—he has keys to both places in England, too. The last secretary left six months ago. It was her complaints which led to the St. Albans police visit.

"They all vanished from different parts of the country. Two lived alone in London, three with their families. It was a long time before the disappearances were connected, and only the other day that we discovered the Geraldine Lorne and Kane connection. They disappeared in exactly the same way—walked out of their homes in the morning, in the usual way, and didn't turn up at their place of business.'

'Peculiar,' said Dawlish, and stirred in his chair. 'What about the other secretaries?'

'We can't trace any others. But she has a new one starting this week. She wants watching very closely.'

Dawlish thought again of Hilda Green.

'And the other branch of this business which you said might lead to violence. How right you were!'

'It's vague,' said Trivett promptly. 'Kane once had a manservant, named Leggett, who'd been in jail twice for crimes of violence. According to what I'm told, Kane knew about it. He left the job a few weeks ago, but—well, I needn't stress the obvious.'

'Explorers who employ ex-convicts with a bad record invite suspicion,' said Dawlish with a yawn. 'Or else he's unlucky with his servants. Like Geraldine. She had a Mr. and Mrs. Parker . . .'

He told Trivett about Parker and everything that had

happened; and while he was there, Trivett put out a call for Parker, with a description. Dawlish did not tell Trivett everything that was in his mind, simply related the facts.

'Who would you prefer to believe—the woman or Rumbold?' Trivett asked.

'I'll keep an open mind, with a slight bias towards Rumbold,' said Dawlish. 'Did you ring Felicity?'

'Oh, yes. She said she supposed I really meant you wouldn't be home to-night.'

'I'll blame everything on to you,' said Dawlish. 'Sorry I haven't been more helpful yet. What's the time?'

It was half-past eight.

'Which explains why I'm hungry,' Dawlish said, and got up.

Trivett chuckled.

'By the way, you'll want these.' He handed Dawlish a sealed envelope. 'Photographs and dossiers of the missing girls.'

Dawlish took a taxi to a restaurant near Higham Mews, where Tim Jeremy had a flat, had a meal which satisfied both his palate and his hunger, and at a quarter to ten left the restaurant for the flat. This was above a large lock-up garage, rented by Tim, and approached by a flight of cement and concrete steps. Higham Mews, near Oxford Street, was a cul-de-sac with a cobbled road surface; in it were several other lock-up garages and two more flats some fifty yards away from Tim's. Tim's main rooms overlooked the mews, but the kitchen and one bedroom were at the back, and had side windows which couldn't be seen from the front because of a chimney stack jutting out from the adjoining building.

A light burned over two garage doors; there were dark corners and shadows, but Dawlish was quickly satisfied that no one lurked in the mews. He had a key; Felicity and he often stayed here, at one time he had shared the flat with Tim. He would call Felicity right away. He jingled the key in his hand as he went quietly up the steps, thrust it into the lock and pushed open the door.

A light shone, at the far end of a small hall.

CHAPTER NINE

HOMELY CHAT

Dawlish stood quite still.

The light shone from a door which stood ajar; the larger of two bedrooms. It showed the hall, the oddments of furniture, and the other door, all of which were closed. There was no sound. He went farther in, closed the front door gently and made sure that the latch didn't click, and, in a darkness relieved only by the light farther along, crept towards the open door.

He stood outside the room.

He heard nothing at first, then a rustle of movement; such as anyone might make who was searching a room.

He waited a few more minutes, and the rustling came again, and then he heard footsteps. He stepped swiftly to one side. The door opened wider, a shadow appeared, and then a hand reached for the light switch, which was outside the door. Even before he saw the hand, Dawlish knew that it was a woman.

He gripped the hand firmly.

A woman cried, '*Oh!*' and terror made her voice shrill.

He switched on the light.

It fell upon Felicity's frightened face, on grey green eyes which were only now losing their fear, on full, well shaped lips. She was not beautiful by accepted standards, but she had beauty to him.

Dawlish shifted his grip on her wrist, drew her to him, hugged and kissed her, then stood back, and smiled.

'Terribly sorry, sweet.'

'You—*terrified* me. I didn't hear a sound.' She drew in a deep breath. 'I—I'll be better in a minute.' she forced a laugh. 'Now I know what it feels like to be on the other side when you're working!'

Her laugh came again and sounded more natural, then faded as swiftly as it had come. She was anxious.

'How's Tim?'

'Fair. You've heard about it?'

'Yes, Gordon of the *Record* telephoned, he heard you'd left the club and thought you'd come home. There was just time to catch the eight-ten, and Trivett seemed doubtful whether you'd really come home. I left a message at the club to tell you I was here, and—well, I am here. I was unpacking—I brought enough clothes for us both.'

They went into the living-room, a large and pleasant room, with a sloping ceiling on one side, and high walls. It had nothing of the splendour of the flat at Hailey Court, but everything that Tim Jeremy was ever likely to require while he remained a bachelor. It wasn't even untidy; he had a good daily woman, who mothered him. On a desk, in the corner, were papers to do with his business affairs, which were not extensive; he lived an active life, had means of his own, and, normally, liked nothing better than working on some affair of mystery and violence with Pat Dawlish.

They had been close friends for twenty years.

Dawlish mixed a weak gin and a strong one, and took them across. Felicity sat in a comfortable arm-chair, Dawlish leaned back on a couch normally large enough for two, actually about the right size for him.

She was frowning, and very serious; and worried.

'How did it start?' she asked.

He told her, simply.

'It all seems so inevitable, when you tell it like that,' conceded Felicity. 'And I know that wild horses and a rogue elephant wouldn't drag you away from it. I suppose I don't really want you to drop it, now that Tim's—' She sipped her drink. 'Have you seen Trivett since?'

'Among several others,' confessed Dawlish, 'and one of them you're going to love.'

He told Felicity everything about his adventures at Hailey Court; and told them so well that half the time she was chuckling, and most of the rest she was smiling. She sat back in her chair, relaxed and easy to look at, and he felt a comfort which he hadn't known since he had heard about Tim.

Felicity said slowly, 'What about these missing girls?'

'Let's have a look at them all together,' said Dawlish, and picked up the large envelope which Trivett had given him. This contained a copy of the dossiers of the missing girls. It also contained a photograph of each one, excellent in every case.

He studied the photographs, with Felicity regarding them without great enthusiasm. Trivett had not exaggerated; they were all out of the ordinary so far as looks were concerned. Two brunettes and three blondes, their ages ranged from twenty-one to twenty-five. He skimmed through the details of their home lives; one had worked in a London typing agency for years—her one break from that had been when she worked for Geraldine Lorne. She was the oldest of the five, a brunette named Marion Grey. The youngest, Loretta Mannion, an orphan, had stage ambitions, and had had a walking-on part in a musical comedy at the time of her disappearance; she was blonde. Doris Hardy was, perhaps, the least outstanding of them all, being inclined to simper in the photograph. Her parents lived in the Midlands, and her father had a good position in one of the large motor-manufacturing companies. Elsa Morgan came from Lancashire, where her parents owned a small chain of dress shops; she was the third blonde. The second brunette and the last on the list was Janet Lisle, the daughter of a manufacturing chemist who lived near Northampton.

The only connecting thread between them was the fact that they had worked for Geraldine Lorne, relinquished the well-paid job—and had also known Sebastian Kane.

'The girls *could* be dead,' Felicity said quietly.

'No bodies found, so far. Bodies do turn up. I didn't talk to Trivett about the obvious, of course.'

'You mean, South America?'

Dawlish chuckled.

'How much you miss! Yes, South America, white slavery, all the usual things one hears about. And that happens. It seems too remote a possibility, we shouldn't think of it but for Kane's knowledge of South America, and that mostly the hinterland.'

'As far as I can tell, you haven't a clue, except where Geraldine Lorne and Kane might lead. You're not convinced about the part they're playing, are you?'

'Care to help in this job?'

Felicity didn't answer.

'I think you could.'

'I suppose you're going to suggest that I could be an attractive bait for Sebastian Kane,' said Felicity, but there was an eager glow in her eyes.

'You could try your hand at another job—friend of Geraldine,' said Dawlish. 'She isn't likely to know you, you could scrape an acquaintance, and it might lead to surprising confidences. In the past, anyone who got to know Geraldine was soon invited to one of her parties, and that wouldn't be a bad idea. There's another line, too. Her new secretary. I've her name and address. You could get to know her, you know how women talk. You've to-morrow to work in, she doesn't start work until the day after to-morrow. Name of Hilda Green, I have it in the little black book. He took the stolen address-book from his pocket. 'That's a job to do to-night—copy these out.'

'All right,' said Felicity; and stifled a yawn. 'Sorry, darling, I don't think I can keep awake any longer. You've tired me out.'

'That's nothing to how tired you're going to be soon,' said Dawlish, with a gleam in his eyes.

She laughed, got up and left him alone. He stood smiling at the door for several seconds, then turned thoughtfully to the telephone.

The news was exactly as Trivett had told him.

He went to Tim's desk, took out some sheets of paper to copy the names from the address-book. They were all men, five in all. Three were in the Home Counties, two actually lived in London, and he might be able to see them next day. He had finished when Felicity looked in, wearing a nylon pyjama suit of apple green.

'That,' she said, 'can wait until morning.'

Thoughts of Geraldine Lorne, Kane, the missing girls, Rumbold, even of Tim, vanished . . .

Felicity lay sleeping.

Dawlish was drowsy, but not yet asleep. Thoughts of the day's events were trickling through his mind again. In these half-wakeful moments ideas sometimes came that could throw a completely new light on to events that had happened during the day.

He heard a car.

It sounded a long way off, and drew nearer; so near, that the snorting seemed to come from the mews outside. Then the engine stopped and a door slammed; no doubt it was one of the cars for the other garages; noisy devils. He heard no voices, but fancied he heard footsteps—and then there was a thunderous knocking at the front door of the flat.

Dawlish got out of bed.

The knocking was like thunder now, and he heard Felicity catch her breath, then heard her gasp:

'What's that? What is it?'

'Visitor,' said Dawlish. 'You stay there, my sweet, I'll soon get rid of the noisy bounder.'

He was in no good mood as he put on his dressing-gown and strode to the door, left it wide open, and reached the front door. He didn't switch on the light. The thunderous knocking was much louder here, and the door was shaking.

He opened it, abruptly.

Kane stood with a hand raised, as if he were going to start thudding again.

CHAPTER TEN

SIX?

Dawlish said icily, 'You're really going to run into trouble soon, Kane. What the devil's the matter?'

Kane didn't answer, but pushed his way into the hall. No one else was in the mews. The big man's figure was a large silhouette against powerful light, because Kane had left his headlamps on, and they bathed the mews in a bright glare. He was breathing heavily, and did not seem in any way aggressive.

Dawlish closed the door, switched on the hall light, and saw Felicity's head poking round the side of the bedroom door. It vanished as soon as he caught sight of it.

Kane was breathing like a grampus.

'What is it?' Dawlish demanded curtly.

Kane gasped, 'She's gone, Dawlish. She's disappeared.'

The light was strong enough to show every feature of his face, and the tiny lines at his eyes and mouth. He was in the middle forties, although at a distance he looked younger, and even at close quarters it was hard to judge his real age, for his hair was jet black without a streak of grey. Anxiety, fear, or some kindred emotion now made him look his age.

'Do you know anything about it?'

'I do not. She was sympathising with you when I left.'

He licked his lips; he wasn't sure what to say, and that might be due to cunning, or it might be because he was really alarmed. 'I had an appointment at nine o'clock. Had to keep it. I was going back to spend the night at Geraldine's. You needn't leer like that!' he roared. 'There's nothing wrong between Geraldine and me! I left at twenty to nine. When I got back, just after eleven, she wasn't there. The flat was empty. I tell you, I'm scared. I thought of you—'

'How did you know where to find me?'

'I asked at the Club, they said you might be here.'

'Why think of me at all?'

'You're up to some funny business,' Kane said. 'I don't trust you that far, Dawlish. Oh, you're honest.' He almost sneered that concession. 'But you might think that Geraldine was mixed up in some nasty business—you hinted at some—and persuade her to come and see you. Is she here?'

'She is not.'

'I'm damned if I believe you,' said Kane. 'I'm going to have a look round.'

He looked as if he expected Dawlish to try to prevent him forcibly from doing that. Dawlish simply stood aside, and said, 'Help yourself,' then he went along to the bedroom. From the open door, he saw that Felicity had already donned a dressing-gown. He winked at her. She came to the door, while Kane was peering into the other rooms.

Kane came out of the kitchen and saw Felicity for the first time. He stopped abruptly, and his scowl disappeared. The ensuing transformation puzzled Dawlish then and for a long time afterwards. Quite suddenly his expression altered, his smile was attractive, he became suave and civil. He looked more impressive too, in greater control of his physical strength.

'My wife,' Dawlish said abruptly. 'Mr. Sebastian Kane.'

Kane bowed.

'Good evening, Mrs. Dawlish. I'm extremely sorry to intrude like this. Your husband's told you why, I suppose.'

'Oh, yes,' she said. 'But perhaps Mrs. Lorne has gone to spend the night with friends. She'd naturally feel a little nervous on her own, wouldn't she?'

'No, Mrs. Dawlish, whatever else, Geraldine isn't nervous. I can't imagine why she should go off without leaving a message for me. No one saw her leave, I can't think where she could have gone. I hoped it would be here.'

'Tried the police?' asked Dawlish.

Kane scowled; became the aggressive and overbearing man again.

'Don't be a fool, man. Of course I haven't. I don't want to raise a scare.'

'I can well understand sweet Geraldine not wanting publicity,' said Dawlish.

Veins stood out on Kane's forehead and neck, and his hands bunched; but with Felicity there, he still retained some semblance of self-control.

'What the devil do you mean by that?'

'I was thinking of a little house near St. Albans.'

'You prying swine,' growled Kane. 'If your wife weren't here, I'd knock you head off your shoulders. Understand this, Dawlish. I won't have you interfering with Mrs. Lorne's private affairs. If I find out that you've persuaded her to leave home, by scaring her, I'll break every bone in your body. Understand?'

He swung on his heel.

The slamming front door shook pictures on the walls and made a draught which sent Felicity's dressing-gown fluttering about her legs.

'Now you know our Sebastian,' murmured Dawlish. 'Nice friendly customer, isn't he?'

'Pat,' Felicity's voice was strained. 'That man hardly knows how to keep going. He's under some great strain, and if his nerve breaks he'll be capable of doing anything. For heaven's sake, be careful with him.'

'Very careful,' Dawlish assured her, and slid an arm round her waist. 'He could be acting, though, couldn't he?'

'Of course he wasn't acting. He's just a bundle of nerves, I shouldn't like to be present when they break.'

'I wonder why he came.'

'To see if Mrs. Lorne was here.'

'Or to make me think that he thought she might be here, which, carried a stage farther, might also have been to make me think that she's number six.'

Felicity said, 'Number six what?'

'Missing girl.'

Felicity said, 'Oh,' in a weak voice. They were in the bedroom, and she sank on to the side of the big, springy, double bed. 'You mean, that he wants to pretend that she's disappeared, and chose this way of doing it.'

'Damsels in danger often disappear, especially if they've a guilty secret and a mind like a cesspool. It would be a nice move on her part. It would suggest that instead of being responsible for the first five disappearances, she's just one of a chain. Add the required touch of cunning, and he would come and tell me about it, because he would be sure that I'd pass it on to the police so they'd know without being officially informed.'

'At times,' said Felicity in a hushed voice, 'you have a devilish mind. You could be right, too. Are you going to tell Trivett?'

'There's no call out for the lady. On the whole, I think it would do more harm than good to tell the police yet.'

'What *are* you going to do?'

'Go to bed,' said Dawlish promptly.

At half-past nine next morning, Dawlish glanced at the notes from Geraldine's address-book, and telephoned Scotland Yard. It was after breakfast, which Felicity had cooked fittingly for a hungry man; Tim's store cupboard was comfortably stocked. The daily woman had arrived, agog and dismayed because of what she had read in the morning papers. Felicity, whom she knew well, had calmed her; they were now together in the kitchen.

The newspapers were on the desk in front of Dawlish, and he glanced at the headlines again as he waited for the call to come through. Tim Jeremy was featured, his photograph appeared, also Rumbold's. He, Dawlish, was mentioned in passing, as a friend of Tim's.

Trivett came on the line.

'Good morning, Pat. Heard from the hospital?'

'Yes. A comfortable night.'

'I should think he's out of danger,' Trivett said reassuringly. 'No need to worry about that, now. How has Felicity taken it?'

'She is going to get to know Miss Hilda Green.'

'Trust Felicity! Although she protests bitterly, secretly I think she enjoys it almost as much as you do.'

'Have you heard from Geraldine or Kane this morning?'

'No, they didn't report Parker's visit. We haven't found Parker, either, or his wife. They lived at Hailey Court, and have no other known address. It's a long job, combing the hotels.'

'Even if they registered as Mr. and Mrs. Parker,' agreed Dawlish. 'Kane looked in late last night, complained bitterly that I was trying to fix a bad reputation on to Geraldine, and also complained that something had scared her and she'd run out on him. Heard anything about that?'

'Why the devil didn't you tell me before?'

'Because she might have turned up during the night,' said Dawlish, 'and I should have hated to call you out of bed on a fool's errand. I'm going to call on her and find out whether she's turned up,' Dawlish went on. 'And that reminds me of the known boy-friends you were so cagey about last night. Any reason why you shouldn't give me their names and addresses?'

'All right,' said Trivett. 'There are only two in London. Reginald Hardy, of 27 Liddel Street, Sloane Square, and Thomas Moor, of The Chalet, 3 Richmond Street, Chelsea.'

Both men were named in Geraldine's address-book.

'Thanks,' said Dawlish, as if he'd known nothing about either of the men. 'Any others?'

Trivett named the three men in the Home Counties, within fairly easy reach of London.

'Thanks again,' said Dawlish. 'Oh, another thing, Bill. Do you know if Geraldine was known much in London during the time she was at St. Albans and in France?'

'She wasn't. She might have been known at hotels, I'm not sure. She doesn't appear to have had a London address, and was staying at the same hotel as the Australian whom she met and married. That's the first time we've traced her. She appeared to be reasonably well off, dressed in the fashion, all that kind of thing.'

Dawlish rang off. He wondered again why Trivett had approached him in the first place; the answer seemed easier to find, now. There were many people in the case who couldn't easily be questioned by the police, but whom he could tackle, passing on anything useful to the Yard.

He dialled the number which he had tried to get twice the previous day, and this time was lucky. A man answered in a deep, abrupt voice.

'*Mister* Beresford, please,' said Dawlish.

'Who—oh, *Pat*! Here, what's up?' The man became excited. 'Why wasn't I in this? How's Tim? I can't get any sense out of the hospital people, this comfortable-night story never seems convincing. Were you in it?' he finished breathlessly.

'Easy.' Dawlish's smile was much broader. 'Yes I am. You are, now. Tim's not doing so badly, either. I tried to get you last night—'

'Was out,' said the man named Beresford, sorrowfully.

'Here are three names and addresses, all of men, all within fifty miles of London,' said Dawlish, carefully. 'The story is simple. They once were friends, in a manner of speaking, of a Mrs. Geraldine Lorne. She set a fast pace, and they didn't last. See if you can find out anything about them, and if you could work a miracle and discover why they parted with Geraldine, it would go in the big book in your favour.'

Dawlish dictated, slowly.

'Hum,' said Beresford heavily. 'Farnham, Maidstone, and Newbury. I doubt if I'll manage them all to-day, but I'll see what I can do. Where do I report?'

'I'm at Tim's.'

'I'll roll up sometime to-night,' promised Beresford.

Dawlish unlocked the bottom drawer of the desk where, he knew, Tim kept a pair of automatics and some ammunition; and he had a licence for the guns. Dawlish took one out, loaded it, slipped it into his pocket, and shrugged at this concession to understandable fears.

Twenty minutes later he was welcomed by a commissionaire outside the Hailey Court flats—a different man from either he had seen the previous evening. It was a bright, sunny morning. One accompanied Dawlish to the door, another took him to the lift, and ignored his protestations that he could find his own way up.

In the morning light, the luxury of the flats was quite as noticeable as by night; there was a hush everywhere, too. The commissionaire, who apparently had no idea that Geraldine Lorne was supposed to be missing, didn't follow him out of the lift. The doors closed with the now familiar muted sound, and the whining started as it went down the shaft.

He opened the front door of the flat with the key he had taken from Geraldine's handbag. The door wasn't bolted. The first thing that surprised him was the electric light, burning in the hall and in one of the rooms; and there was no daylight, nothing to suggest that the curtains had been drawn. So Geraldine wasn't back, and Kane hadn't worried about switching off the lights.

He went to the drawing-room.

He stopped dead, on the threshold.

A girl lay on the floor, by the front of the couch. One hand was raised and resting on the couch in an odd position. Her body was limp and her head lolled against the cushion, which had been dragged to the floor.

Her lips were parted, her eyes were open slightly and had a glazed look. Before he moved again, he knew that she was dead, and had died by strangulation.

CHAPTER ELEVEN

POOR LORETTA

Dawlish did not go to the dead girl at once, but went into the other rooms; each was empty. The handbag from which he had taken the key was gone. There was no sign anywhere of burglary or of a search. Profound quiet filled the flat, as if the inanimate things knew of the shadow of death.

Dawlish went back to the drawing-room.

He had seen the dead girl's picture; she was one of the five missing secretaries.

This was Loretta Mannion. He touched her wrist; it was cold, although the central heating and the closed windows made the room warm. She had been dead for many hours. Her arm did not move at his touch, because of the stiffness of *rigor mortis*. There was nothing really ugly about her appearance; just vacancy of expression. What ugliness there was showed in the shadowy patches on her throat: bruises.

Apart from this, the room was much as he had left it the night before. There were two extra glasses. A half-smoked cigar lay on an ash-tray. The tea-things had been cleared away. Another chair had been used, judging from the rumpled cushion; poor Loretta's chair?

He went across to the telephone, touched the receiver, but did not lift it. Trivett was almost certainly sitting in his office; would take the call and come straight here, with his battery of assistants. The affairs of Geraldine Lorne, shrouded until then in mystery and handled with such secrecy, would glow in the spotlight of high-powered publicity. Trivett would not be able to keep this from the Press, and probably wouldn't want to.

Dawlish took his hand away from the receiver.

He moved away from the telephone and looked down at the dead girl. It was easy to imagine how pretty she had been in life. It was equally easy to imagine that the other four had suffered death, like this. She was well-dressed, well-cared for, there was no hint of ordeal or privations; she had simply come to 31 Hailey Court, and been murdered. He found himself wondering if it would be wise to keep this discovery from both police and Press, for the time being. He examined the position, from all points of view. It was a serious offence; he'd committed worse a dozen times while driving towards a solution of some mystery. It might lose precious time for the police, in their investigation; that was where the gamble came in, he thought it possible that results would come more quickly if the body were concealed.

It would be a characteristic gambit, born of the idea that the girl's body had been left here, simply to make sure that it was found; to make sure that Geraldine Lorne was forced into the spotlight and also forced into close contact with the police.

That theory made Geraldine a possible victim of conspiracy.

What would Trivett think of that?

He'd probably go up in the air, call Dawlish a thousand times a fool, say that the sprite had bewitched him as she had so many big men. He would say that Kane and Geraldine had killed Loretta Mannion and taken flight; that Kane's visit to

Dawlish's flat had been an effort to get Dawlish to go there the previous night, and so see for himself that the flat was empty and Geraldine gone. That would provide a kind of alibi for Geraldine Lorne—and Trivett would undoubtedly say that Kane had wanted to provide one.

Trivett, in fact, would set the police hounds after Geraldine and her champion, and their disappearance would convince police, Press, and public of their guilt.

Dawlish picked up the receiver and dialled a Kensington number which he'd learned off by heart the previous night: Kane's. There was no immediate answer.

Dawlish kept the receiver to his ear for several seconds after he'd given up hope of getting a reply, replaced it, stared blankly at the wall, then dialled another number. A man answered him, respectfully.

'This is the Carilon Club.'

'Good morning,' said Dawlish. 'Is Mr. Kane in residence.'

'One moment, sir, and I'll find out. Who is speaking?'

'Patrick Dawlish.'

From where he stood, Dawlish could see the top of Loretta Mannion's head and the hand which lodged against the couch. Another head seemed to replace it, of fluffy brown hair. It was easy to picture Geraldine Lorne tripping about the flat, *petite* and delightful. Yes, he had to admit it; delightful.

When he'd questioned her, fear had entered her heart, and at times he had thought she was putting on an act.

He hadn't paid much attention to it then; had been more concerned with the possibility that Rumbold had lied about where he'd taken his orders, but—

'Yes, sir, Mr. Kane is in residence,' said the operator at the Carilon Club. 'I am having him paged for you. Will you please hold on?'

* * *

He heard sundry mutterings on the line, then the quiet was broken by Kane's gruff voice.

'You there, Dawlish?'

''Morning, Kane,' said Dawlish, as if nothing had happened to make them bad friends. 'Has Mrs. Lorne turned up?'

'No. I'm as worried as hell. Hardly slept. I've called her flat half a dozen times this morning, and there's no answer.'

'Tried her friends?'

'She hadn't any friends she was likely to stay with in London,' said Kane. 'I tell you something's happened to her. Did you tell the police last night?'

'No.'

'So you've some sense,' said Kane, and was obviously relieved. 'Look here, Dawlish, I want to see you. No point in two intelligent men being at loggerheads, we can probably help each other. You can help me more than I can help you,' he conceded, with obvious reluctance. 'When can you meet me?'

'Luncheon. At the Club.'

'Not before?'

'Sorry, no. You say that she didn't have friends in London whom she might stay with. What about friends outside?'

'She cut herself off from her friends, after that stinking business at St. Albans,' Kane said.

'Did you go back to Hailey Court last night?'

'Yes. Stayed there until after one o'clock. Just couldn't settle. Place is like a morgue if Geraldine isn't there. So I came on here, telling the porters to call me if she turned up.'

'I see,' said Dawlish. 'Look here, wait at the Club. If I can get there earlier than lunch-time, I will. I may be in a hurry.'

'I won't stay here two minutes, if I get news of Geraldine,' declared Kane, forthrightly.

'That's understood. Leave word telling me where you've gone, though, won't you?' said Dawlish abruptly, and rang off.

The most likely man to call here was Kane. Trivett and the police weren't likely to come. There were no servants; Hilda Green wasn't due until to-morrow. The simple thing to do with the body was to hide it here. Twelve hours should be sufficient, twenty-four hours certainly would be.

He went into the bedroom and examined the wardrobe with its three partitions. Only Geraldine Lorne was likely to want to look in the wardrobe. There were keys in the locks. He shifted some clothes and made plenty of room for Loretta Mannion's body to rest; it would have to be sitting up, she couldn't lie flat. He went back for her, and lifted her; it was strange to hold that stiff body, to know that he couldn't easily alter the position of the arms and legs. He eased her in; and as luck would have it, there was room for her in exactly the position which he had found her. He pushed her dress in, then closed and locked the door; he also locked the two other doors in the wardrobe, and pocketed the keys. All the time he used a handkerchief; to avoid leaving prints.

Then he went into the drawing-room and poured himself a stiff whisky; he needed it.

Two bright and breezy commissionaires saluted him as he went off.

He was tired of hiring taxis, so went to a motor-hire firm where he was well known and hired a Jaguar with plenty of speed; a gleaming black monster. He drove at once to 27 Liddel Street, Sloane Square. This was a tall, narrow house in a narrow grey street, a backwater of London. It was divided into three flats; and the top flat was tenanted by Mr. Reginald Hardy, one of the men who was known to have been on 'friendly' terms with Geraldine Lorne. A manservant opened the door.

'Good morning, sir.'

'Is Mr. Hardy in?'

'I'm afraid not, sir,' said the man. 'In fact I'm rather worried about him, he hasn't been home for two nights. I've had no message. It's not unusal for him to stay away a night without informing me, but two nights—he usually sends some message. Are you—are you a friend of his, sir?'

'A friend of a friend,' said Dawlish, and looked worried because that was likely to impress the man. 'It's puzzling, isn't it? And I'm anxious to see him, I've a message for him.'

'I'll pass it on, sir, as soon as I hear from Mr. Hardy.'

'Er—yes. Yes, that would do. On the other hand, it's a confidential matter.' Dawlish looked even more worried. 'I think the best thing is to ask him to get in touch with Mrs. Geraldine Lorne as soon as you can.'

'Mrs. Lorne!' ejaculated the man. 'Has that woman—I *beg* your pardon, sir.' He hesitated before going on: 'I have had strict instructions never to admit Mrs. Lorne to the flat, and to ignore telephone messages from her. In fact, sir, I know that Mr. Hardy has destroyed her recent letters, without opening them. I'm sorry, sir.'

'Oh, that's all right. I'm just the messenger. Didn't know I might tread on corns.' Dawlish looked almost inane. 'Worrying about Mr. Hardy, though. Very worrying, especially for you.'

The man bowed distantly—and watched him from the front window as he climbed into the Jaguar.

Dawlish was ten minutes getting to The Chalet, 3 Richmond Road, Chelsea, the home of Mr. Thomas Moor, and spent the ten minutes wondering about two things; the barrier which Hardy had put up against sweet Geraldine and the fact that Hardy was missing.

The Chalet was small, charming, and modern. It had a small

garden, the lawn was trim, everything seemed spick-and-span. In a pram in the loggia was a tiny infant.

A maid answered his ring.

'Is Mr. Moor in?' asked Dawlish pleasantly.

'Oh, *no*, sir, he's not, he—'

'All right, Muriel,' said another woman.

She came from the side of the hall, and had obviously been standing by, to listen. She was tall and, in her well-groomed, rather aloof way, attractive—a brunette in the middle thirties.

'Good morning,' she said. 'I am Mrs. Moor.'

''Morning,' beamed Dawlish. 'Sorry if I'm being a nuisance, but I've a message for Mr. Moor, I understood he would be at home.'

'He has been away for several days,' said Mrs. Moor. She looked as if she meant that her husband had been missing for several days. 'May I pass on the message?'

'Well, I don't know. It's a bit difficult. Er—from Mrs. Lorne, Mrs. Geraldine—'

The woman backed away as if he'd struck her.

CHAPTER TWELVE

MISSING MEN

Mrs. Moor recovered quickly. Self-control prevented her from voicing the rage which surged through her mind.

'I will tell my husband,' she said icily.

'Thanks,' burbled Dawlish. 'Nice of you. I know it's urgent. You see—'

'Good morning,' said Mrs. Moor, and began to close the door; but it wouldn't close, for Dawlish's foot was in the way. Her eyes flashed again, and the maid, who had been hovering in a doorway, stared with popping eyes. 'Will you please take your foot away!' Mrs. Moor's voice was like ice.

Dawlish dropped the inanity, and his expression puzzled her, the flare of anger faded.

'Sorry,' said Dawlish. 'This is really important, isn't it? I'm no friend of Mrs. Lorne. Is your husband missing?'

She didn't answer.

Dawlish took out a card.

'My name's Dawlish. It might mean something to you, from the newspapers. Patrick Dawlish.'

'Are you *the* Patrick Dawlish? The man who is mentioned in the newspapers this morning?'

'I'm afraid so.'

'Come in,' she said, abruptly.

The maid had disappeared from the doorway, and Mrs. Moor led Dawlish to a small, beautifully appointed drawing-room.

'I am just going to have some coffee, will you join me?'

She rang a bell.

'Please sit down.' The maid appeared and she added, 'Bring coffee, Muriel, please.'

Inwardly, he judged, she was afire with anxiety, reft by emotions which tormented her.

'Why have you come?' she asked.

'Let me put it this way. Curious things have happened to friends of Mrs. Lorne, and I'm trying to find out why. Unofficially, of course.'

'Is it connected with the attack on your friend?'

Framing that question took courage; and she was afraid of the answer. That surely meant that she had reason to fear violence.

'It could be,' he said. 'No more than that. This is in strict confidence, of course.'

'Of course. What makes you think it might be connected?'

'My friend was going to see another friend of Mrs. Lorne's,' said Dawlish. 'Of course, it could have nothing to do with her. Probably hasn't. On the other hand, the Mrs. Lorne angle is there, and I want to follow it. You're worried about your husband, aren't you?'

'He hasn't been home for three days,' she said.

'Have you reported it?'

'No,' she said, and looked at the door. The maid brought in the coffee, and couldn't keep her eyes off Dawlish. She went out quickly, and closed the door with a snap. 'No,' repeated Mrs.

Moor. 'I haven't felt justified in reporting it.' She picked up the coffee-pot. 'My husband and I had a sharp difference of opinion just before he left. It is possible that he's not returned because of that. It was about Mrs. Lorne. I knew of their association before our marriage, of course, and the matter was seldom discussed. Three days ago, I discovered that he was still in touch with her. We quarrelled bitterly. He went out, without packing a bag, without saying where he was going, and I've heard nothing since. You will understand why I haven't wanted to report it.'

'Yes, of course.' Dawlish took his coffee and helped himself to coffee-sugar crystals. 'I don't think it was because of the quarrel, Mrs. Moor.'

Hope flared and died, and was replaced by dread, but she didn't speak.

'Another old friend of Mrs. Lorne's has been missing for two or three days,' Dawlish said. 'He wasn't married, so there wasn't a quarrel. Forgive me, Mrs. Moor, but one man has died another has been badly injured, still more may be in danger. Your husband, possibly—I don't know, but I hope you'll tell me everything you can about his association with Mrs. Lorne.'

She didn't answer at once; and he was content to wait. At last she spoke in a low-pitched voice from which she tried to exclude all feeling.

'I know very little about it, but understand that she is an exceptionally attractive woman, with unpleasant pastimes. I understood that the association was completely finished, and it shocked me when I discovered that it wasn't.'

'How did you discover that?'

'He had a letter from her,' she said. 'Her name and a crest were on the envelope.'

'Did you read the letter?'

'No.'

'When did it arrive?'

'By the midday post, on Monday.' That was four days ago. 'My husband didn't come in until a little after six o'clock. I gave him the letter. He read it, put it in his pocket, and said nothing. I—well, we quarrelled, and he went out. Since then I have been tormented by—'

Dawlish said gently, 'Tormented by the possibility that she sent for him, isn't that it? And that her hold was so strong that he couldn't resist.'

She didn't speak.

Dawlish said, 'May I make one or two assumptions? That you are deeply attached to your husband, and believed that he was, to you? That this was a ghost of the past which you thought had been exorcised—and it shocked you beyond words when you realised that it hadn't. That you took up an attitude because you felt that he had betrayed you, and because you were afraid that he wasn't as deeply attached as you'd believed. And that since then you have been tormented, because you don't know what to believe. You're frightened in case harm has come to him, an accident while he was in a rage, perhaps—and equally frightened, in case he walked out quite coldly and deliberately. And won't come back. There's an explanation that you haven't thought of, you know. That she may have used some pressure on him, to make him go to see her. I'll put it crudely. Blackmail.'

'Have you any reason to think—'

'No reason, I'm guessing. Have you seen any indication that he might have been blackmailed? Anything to suggest that he was spending more money than usual, or that he was worried?'

'Yes,' she said, slowly. 'He *was* worried. He hadn't been himself for several weeks. It started after a burglary we had here about two months ago. The safe was opened, but my jewels weren't in it, and little was stolen. It made him nervous and irritable, and he's never really been himself again. He complained of head-aches frequently, and I wanted him to see a doctor. He told me that he hated the moods when they caught him, that he was fighting against them. I couldn't understand it, unless he was actually ill.'

'And the blackmail possibility?'

'He's said nothing about it. I can't imagine that he would be very worried by that, even if he paid money. He is very— he could afford anything within reason. No, I don't think he would be worried by blackmail, he might be angry about it. Mr. Dawlish, be frank with me. Have you any reason to think that anything has happened to Tom?'

Dawlish said, 'You'd be the last to want me to pretend that the possibility doesn't exist. You may recall something which would help us to find out what's been worrying him, and if it had to do with Mrs. Lorne, the sooner I know the better. Meanwhile—do you want to tell the police, now?'

'I'll leave that to your discretion,' she said. He left, twenty minutes later, and she saw him to the door. He glanced back, from the car. She was standing by the pram. She didn't look towards Dawlish as he let in the clutch and drove off.

'Yes, Pat?' said Trivett, on the telephone.

'Did you know that Reginald Hardy and Thomas Moor have been missing for three days?'

'I did not!'

'Well, they have. Possibly they've been hypnotised by Geraldine Lorne. Anything new about her?'

'No. What about Kane?'

'I'm going to have lunch with him,' said Dawlish, from the call box near Chelsea Town Hall. 'Anything else your end?'

'No. Pat, are you sure about these men?'

'Positive. I plead no immediate action, certainly no publicity.'

'Come and see me after you've talked to Kane, will you?' asked Trivett. 'And Pat, don't keep anything up your sleeve. After what happened in Soho. I'm prepared to believe anything.'

'Do you know anything off hand about a burglary at Moor's house in Chelsea, two months ago?'

'Funny you should mention that,' said Trivett. 'One of my men told me about it to-day. It was a Divisional job, of course. We didn't handle it. A straightforward job by a regular safe-breaker. Nothing much was stolen. Why do you ask?'

'He was a changed man after it,' said Dawlish. 'I fancy he lost more than he told the police or his wife.'

He rang off soon afterwards, contemplating the crowded King's Road, which was twenty yards from this narrow street where he had found a telephone kiosk.

He dialled Tim's flat.

Felicity answered, promptly.

'Pat? Pat, listen. I've had a message from Ted. He rang up to say that the first man he called on is missing. He's going after the others as fast as he can. He telephoned from Newbury. Apparently the man he was to see there disappeared, three days ago. He just left his home one morning, and didn't come back. He didn't take any clothes with him, told no one he was plan-ning to stay away. Pat, what *is* happening?'

'Where's Ted going next?'

'I'm not sure. He said he'd be in time for tea.

'Give him a good one, he deserves it,' said Dawlish. 'Goodbye, my sweet. I'll be back about three.'

He rang off, before she could ask questions, and glanced out of the kiosk. He had noticed no one following him that morning, and the small man who leaned against the wall a few yards along might simply be waiting for the telephone. Dawlish glanced at him, gave a semi-apologetic smile as he stepped out, and walked straight on, towards his car, which was near the corner.

He drew level with the man.

He saw something poke against the man's coat pocket; and it might be a gun.

CHAPTER THIRTEEN

ATTACK

Dawlish did not appear to pay much attention to the man. Instead, he glanced across the road. A small car stood there, facing the far end of the street, its back to the main road. He was now nearly level with the lounging man. He dropped his right hand to his pocket and the automatic which Felicity had persuaded him to take.

He passed the man.

He jumped forward.

The muffled roar of a shot rang out. He saw neither flame nor smoke, but the man was no longer leaning against the wall, he was running across the road towards the little car. Dawlish fell against a lamp-post. The little man, hands in sight, reached the car. The driver started the engine, as Dawlish straightened up. The driver was looking at him, and showing a gun.

Dawlish fired.

He hit a rear tyre, there was a sharp, explosive sound and a loud hiss. Then he flung himself backwards, for the driver also fired. A bullet chipped pieces out of the wall. The man who had been lounging realised what had happened to the car, turned and raced towards the far end of the street. The driver, as if in sudden panic, flung open the door and fired twice towards Dawlish, but was careless with his aim. Dawlish wasn't. Dawlish's second bullet caught the man in the leg and sent him down, gun flying from his hand. The first gunman was too far away for deadly shooting; Dawlish raced after him.

A police whistle shrilled out. Two policemen reached the corner and came running, a few passers-by joined them. As Dawlish ran a crowd gathered about the entrance to the narrow street, and traffic was held up. Dawlish didn't glance round, but gained quickly on the man who had been lying in wait, and saw him turn, with the gun ready to shoot. Dawlish kept going. He heard the bark of the report and saw the flash, this time, and didn't know how near the bullet came. The man turned and raced away again, as if he knew that he hadn't much chance of scoring a hit.

A car turned a corner, some way ahead.

The man saw it, stopped, darted to one side, tripped against the kerb and fell; and his gun slid from his grasp and hit against the wall of a house. Before he had recovered his breath, Dawlish was on him. The startled motorist pulled up, and two policemen came thudding along the street.

Dawlish picked up his assailant's gun, and was looking down at the man when the police came up.

It took Dawlish half an hour to convince the Chelsea police that they should telephone Trivett at the Yard; after that, they became affable and helpful, and told him that he could do exactly what he liked. The two prisoners, one bruised and the other with a shattered knee, were on the way to the nearest hospital; and Yard men were also on the way, to question them. They were both young, in the early twenties; just two desperadoes—with specific orders?

It would be some time before Dawlish knew about that.

Sergeant-Major Vye saluted him.

'Hallo, Sam. Anything to report?'

'Not a thing, sir.'

Dawlish went up the circular staircase towards the cocktail bar and the dining-room—the cocktail bar was a recent innovation, and still shunned by the majority of club members over sixty.

Kane was propped up against the bar, glowering, talking to no one. Half a dozen other members were standing some distance off, as if they did not want to rub shoulders with the explorer. Kane was watching the door, and moved abruptly when he saw Dawlish.

'I thought you'd never come,' he growled. 'It's ten past one.'

They went to a small table, where the bar-keeper brought drinks, so small that it looked as if two adults had strayed into a kindergarten.

Kane's scowl was dark, giving him an almost sinister look.

'Any news?'

'Afraid not,' said Dawlish. 'That is, not about Geraldine.'

'I'm not interested in any other news,' said Kane. 'Dawlish, tell me—why did you come to see Geraldine?'

'Because the dead Rumbold said he'd received orders from her. I had to check.'

'Once and for all, it was a lie. She didn't know Rumbold. After you'd gone last night, she told me so. And she was scared out of her wits, poor kid.'

'I can imagine. Where did you take her?'

Kane's hands bunched on the table.

'What the hell do you mean by that?'

'Look here, old chap, I know that you're stewing in a kind of hell because Geraldine's in trouble. That sticks out a mile. Where did you take her?'

'Nowhere. I told you the truth.'

'And you still haven't the slightest idea where she might be?'

'No.'

'Still unwilling to go to the police?'

Kane didn't answer, and the liaison-waiter came up to say that a table was free. They followed him, and as they reached the dining-room, many eyes were turned towards them, for they were the two largest members of the club, and together they were formidable.

The table was in a window, and there was a pillar behind it, a window on one side; it was one of the most secluded in the huge room. When they had ordered and the waiter had gone, he looked at Dawlish in much the same way as he had looked at Felicity the night before.

'Geraldine's in danger. She's had something on her mind for weeks. I've spotted it, but she wouldn't talk about it, just said it was nonsense. First time I've seen her scared was last night. After you'd gone. Apparently when you said that Rumbold had received orders from her, it shook her badly.'

'Did she know what had happened to Rumbold?' asked Dawlish mildly.

'Yes.'

'How?'

'*I* don't know. And from the moment you left, she was scared out of her wits. Never seen her like it. I had to leave—hated it, but just had to. She seemed a bit better, and I'd given her a drink. She locked herself in when I'd gone, said she'd go to bed. When I got back—she was gone.'

'And you don't know why?'

Kane drew in a deep breath.

'She's afraid of the police. Don't know why! Can't understand it. The one thing I do know, Dawlish, is that she's done nothing to be ashamed of—not deliberately, anyhow. All that nonsense about what happened at St. Albans—it makes me sick. Well, there it is. Geraldine obviously thinks someone is after her. For all she knew, you might go straight to the police and tell them this lie that Rumbold told you, so—she left. Don't blame her, but—I've got to find her. Can't do it myself, can't go to the police, so—that's why I want your help. If you've any decency in you, you'll give it. Well, what about it?' Kane asked abruptly.

CHAPTER FOURTEEN

THE WARDROBE

Dawlish glanced at the man's hands, which were on the table, fingers crooked; and he thought, as he had before, that there was sufficient strength in them to squeeze the life out of anyone.

'I'll do what I can, but you'll have to tell me everything you know.'

A waiter brought game pie.

A page with ash blond hair made a bee-line for their table.

'There's a lady on the telephone for you, Mr. Kane! A Mrs. Lorne, sir.'

Kane jumped up, sent his chair crashing back, pushed the lad aside, and strode out of the dining-room; the glares which followed him were undoubtedly hostile. Dawlish brushed the back of his hair as the boy picked the chair up, and the waiter, quite unperturbed, began to serve the pie.

'I doubt if I'll need that,' said Dawlish. 'If Mr. Kane comes back, tell him I had a message and had to hurry off, will you?'

He passed the telephone booths, and saw Kane standing and staring straight in front of him, ignoring the passage; Kane's lips were set in a smile.

Sergeant-Major Vye saluted.

'Nothing to report, sir.'

'Thanks. Let me have a word with the telephone operator, will you?'

The operator was in a cubby-hole behind the porter's desk, an elderly man.

'That call for Mr. Kane,' said Dawlish. 'Is it local or long distance?'

'Oh, local, sir.'

Dawlish hurried out and to his car, and was out of sight before Kane had appeared. Dawlish drove straight to Hailey Court, but side-tracked the commissionaires by entering at the back entrance. An old man who was cleaning shoes looked up in surprise—and smiled back at Dawlish's beaming face. Dawlish found the service lift and went up to the third floor, strode along it to Number 31, and opened the door with his key.

He heard a movement.

He stepped inside, closing the door without a sound; someone appeared to be in the kitchen. He tip-toed to the hall wardrobe, which was tall but not quite tall enough for him. He bent his head and stepped inside, the door creaked a little, but there was no comment from whoever was at home. He had to crouch low, and he waited patiently, ears strained to catch the slightest sound.

The first he heard was of footsteps, outside the door.

Then someone ran lightly, as lightly as Geraldine Lorne was likely to run, towards the door. A moment later Kane boomed:

'Honey, thank God you're back!'

Dawlish didn't know what followed, but could guess; and the guessing was helped by a little gasp, as if the girl were unable to keep quiet beneath Kane's bear-hug.

A door closed.

'What in heaven's name happened to you, pet? Was Dawlish behind it?'

Geraldine's voice came promptly, unflurried, and with a hint of gaiety in it.

'No, of course not. Seb, don't worry me with questions now, I just had to go and—and see someone. I'm all right. I knew you wouldn't approve and would try to stop me from going, so I had to slip out when you'd left. And I couldn't get back last night. I'm sorry, sweet. I'm glad you came at once, Seb—'

'Any time you call, I'll come. You've only got to call.'

Another sound came; a kiss?

Dawlish ventured to open the door an inch, and peered into the hall. The two were at the open door of the bedroom. They disappeared.

Dawlish stepped out of the wardrobe. He had learned most of what he wanted to learn, and it did not reflect to Kane's discredit; the girl remained a complete mystery. He strode softly to the door, and could just see inside. Kane had a great arm round Geraldine. He watched as the girl broke away, and went to the wardrobe.

She would find it locked.

Geraldine pulled the handle of the door, and it opened.

Dawlish had the keys in his pocket.

The door opened wide, Geraldine looked inside, and turned to Kane with a ravishing smile.

'Be a darling,' Geraldine said. 'I must change into a different dress, this one's *fright*ful. I won't be long.'

She stretched her arms inside, for a dress.

Kane turned round immediately, said, 'Sure, honey,' and strode out of the room. As he came, Dawlish moved backwards towards the kitchen door. Kane turned towards the drawing-room, and went inside. Dawlish hovered at the kitchen door as Geraldine closed that of the bedroom. Kane picked up the telephone; Dawlish heard the bell *ting*. From there, Kane couldn't see into that part of the hall between Dawlish and the front door.

Dawlish reached the door, as Kane said:

'Carilon Club? Give Mr. Dawlish a message, please—my apologies, and Mrs. Lorne is quite all right. That's all.'

Dawlish stepped outside, closed the front door softly. He went past the lift, walked down the stairs, strode out, took the wheel of his car, and drove towards Scotland Yard.

Trivett had two men with him, young detective officers who had seen Dawlish only at a distance. They were introduced, and Trivett let them talk for a minute or two; actually allowed them time to appraise Dawlish before they left. When the door closed, he pushed cigarettes across the desk, smiled wryly, and said:

'So you're really in one piece.'

Dawlish looked at him through a cloud of smoke.

'Results?'

'Not satisfactory,' said Trivett. 'They're young brutes—there are too many like them about. One of these was inside for twelve months, for robbery. The other hasn't a record, but what we've discovered about him since suggests he ought to have had. They're a couple of desperadoes, with guns, and they've pulled off two nasty robberies in the past few weeks—we've pinned those on to them. They'll do anything for money. All they'll say about this morning's job is that they were paid to put you away,' Trivett said quietly.

'Did they say how they came to find me there?'

'They'd followed you from the garage where you got the car. They lost you at Sloane Square, but picked you up again in

Chelsea, and when you went to that telephone booth you made a sitting bird. They thought it was going to be easy.'

'You haven't been able to make them say who gave them the job?'

'No. Each had a hundred pounds in one-pound notes in his wallet, and said they were paid in advance. We may be able to trace the notes, although they're all old, it won't be easy.'

'It's getting interesting. I told you about Moor and Hardy, didn't I? Now Ted's discovered that . . .'

It did not take him long to tell Trivett of the other man who had vanished from his home. Trivett telephoned to the police-station near the home of the man, asked them to make what inquiries they could, begged them to send him news as soon as it came; and added:

'See if you can find any recent connection between him and Geraldine Lorne, will you?'

When he rang off, he looked hard into Dawlish's eyes, and said softly:

'That woman's a devil. Are you sure she's missing?'

'She was. She isn't. She came back about an hour ago—a little more, probably.'

'To Hailey Court?'

'Yes.'

'Damn and blast the fools!' exploded Trivett. 'I've had the flats watched, I told them I wanted a report the moment she turned up.' He lifted the telephone fiercely. 'I want a patrol car to pick up Sergeant Hennessey at Hailey Court, and to bring him back here at once. Hurry.'

He replaced the receiver; Dawlish had seldom seen him looking more annoyed.

'Hennessey—don't I know him? Biggish, fair-haired, chunk of a chin, and quite a sense of humour. Goes in for pigeon racing, or something like that. Sound chap,' reflected Dawlish. 'I shouldn't think he would make a slip of this kind, would you?'

'It's not like him,' Trivett said, and frowned. 'Now what's in your mind? You haven't had some silly idea of bluffing me, have you? She did disappear.'

'Positively. I know she wasn't anywhere in the flat this morning, I'm not simply taking Kane's word for it.'

'You can't take Kane's word for anything,' said Trivett. 'I don't suppose you've missed one obvious possibility, Pat. Tim and Rumbold were strangled, and from the marks on their throats, by a man with pretty big fingers and powerful hands. There's a lot of bruising at the wind-pipe but little at the back of the neck, which suggested that the pressure was localised. A man with big hands might squeeze like that and have the heels of his thumbs pressing against each other—that would prevent bruising at the back. So far, we haven't discovered where Kane was at the time this happened, but we know he wasn't at his flat or at the Carilon Club or at Geraldine Lorne's flat.'

'He's obviously a possible, but so far I can't imagine why,' said Dawlish. 'Now let me ask a question. Have you any idea what Geraldine Lorne is up to? Is your interest only because of the missing girls, or did it start before that?'

'You know everything I know,' Trivett assured him. 'I wish—'

The telephone bell rang, and he answered it quickly, was held in conversation for several minutes, and then had to leave the office. Dawlish waited for nearly a quarter of an hour, letting thoughts trickle through his mind, and his eyes were half-closed when the door opened and Trivett and Detective Sergeant Hennessey came in, Trivett striding, Hennessey frowning.

Trivett said, 'Pat, are you sure the woman's in the flat? Hennessey swears she hasn't gone in while he's been watching. We had a man at the back, too, who's quite as certain.'

CHAPTER FIFTEEN

SUCCESS FOR FELICITY

At ten minutes to four, Dawlish opened the door of Tim's flat, and heard a man say in a deep voice:

'Never worry about Patrick Dawlish. Nothing will stop him from dying in his bed,' declared the man with the deep voice, who was Ted Beresford. Dawlish stepped softly to the door of the living-room, looking round it, and saw Felicity sitting on the arm of a chair, dressed in a leopard-skin coat, a small brown hat trimmed with the same fur, and a pair of crocodile shoes. She was swinging her right leg against the side of the chair, impatiently.

Beresford, also a big man, sat back in the largest chair, his left leg bent and his right stretched straight out in front of him. It was artificial; he had lost a leg in what he liked to call one of Dawlish's little peccadilloes. He was bulky, dark-haired, and untidy. He smoked a pipe with a huge bowl, and smoke billowed up from it. In repose, as now, he was ugly.

'Anyone at home?' asked Dawlish pipingly.

'Pat!' Felicity jumped up. 'You're late!'

Felicity hurried across to the door.

'I think I've found someone who knows Hilda Green, and I'm due at Cherry's for tea at four, I must hurry. Everything all right?'

'Yes. Provided you don't buy the evening papers.'

'What's happened?'

'Nasty men with guns, doing all the wrong things. You'll be followed from the front door to Cherry's and back again by a large policeman—youngish, and he keeps carrier pigeons. Name of Hennessey.'

'Oh, Pat,' said Felicity.

'Care to forget all about Hilda? It's a long chance, and it could possibly get you into more trouble than either of us will want.'

Beresford sat upright in his chair; tensely.

Felicity said, 'Oh, I'll go on with it.'

She turned and hurried out, and the door slammed.

Dawlish glanced at Beresford, smiled tautly, and stepped to the window. Hennessey was waiting outside, and walked in Felicity's wake. Dawlish turned to look at his friend. Beresford, frowning, was even uglier. Dawlish went to the chair which Felicity had been using, and sat on the same arm.

'Thanks, Ted.'

'Forget it. Need to put the wind up Fel?'

'Yes.'

'Pity,' grunted Beresford. 'I had a nasty feeling that it might blow pretty strong. Three missing men are no joke. Felicity told me something about the damsels, too.'

'Did you say *three*?'

'Oh, yes. Same reports at Maidstone and Farnham as at Newbury. The men simply vanished.'

Dawlish went to the telephone, called the Yard and, as Trivett wasn't in, left a message about this news. Beresford went on, almost as if there had been no pause.

'This Geraldine Lorne and her love-life?'

'Fel's certainly been talking! Feel in a receptive mood?' asked Dawlish, and slid off the arm into the chair. For the first time since the affair had started he took out his pipe and began to fill it.

'Fire away,' Beresford said.

He had a trick of listening intelligently, and next to Felicity, was the best audience Dawlish knew.

The telling took nearly forty minutes, and the only sounds which came from Beresford were little puffing noises as he blew out smoke, and an occasional grunt.

He finished.

'Hum,' said Beresford. 'Pretty little tale, isn't it? Only contact with the villains of the piece seem to be sweet Geraldine and Kane. And the odd-job men.'

Dawlish nodded.

'Of course, you've seen the obvious possibility following Hennessey's report,' said Beresford, lazily.

'I think so,' said Dawlish. 'If Hennessey said she didn't go into the flats, she certainly didn't go in as herself. We had quite a chat. No closed car drew up, and only a few women went in, none of them measuring up to Geraldine's shape or size in the slightest degree. The man at the back, also a good chap, was equally certain. So—'

'No disguise,' said Beresford.

'Apparently not. Unless she went in as a man. Much easier than as a woman,' Dawlish remarked. 'There were two small men, but Hennessey didn't see either of them come out.'

'Knocked my suggestion for six,' said Beresford.

'It hasn't, and you haven't made it yet. I don't know whether Trivett's seen it—I can't believe he'd miss it, although he certainly didn't give a hint. She may not have gone far. To another flat at Hailey Court, in fact—that what you're thinking?'

Beresford took his pipe from his lips—and nodded.

'And the body could have been taken to this second flat,' said Dawlish.

Again Beresford nodded, and Dawlish didn't speak for a few minutes, just sat back and drew at his pipe. Beresford looked as if he were half-asleep. He opened one eye wide, and said: 'What's next for me to do?'

'You might nip around and find out what you can about Hardy, Moor, and their friends,' said Dawlish. 'And more about their association with Geraldine. Be careful, because they'll probably know you're in it with me.'

Beresford said, 'Yes. Pat, if you're so close that they want to bump you off, can't you see what you're close to?'

'It could be Hardy or Moor,' said Dawlish. 'Look at it this way—the gunmen lost me at Sloane Square and picked me up again at Chelsea. Normally, I shouldn't come to Chelsea from there. If I'd just gone to make a single call, I'd come back to the West End. They decided to try Chelsea. What's more. I was off the main road for some time, I must have been with Mrs. Moor for three-quarters of an hour. Yet they picked me up without any difficulty at all.'

'Meaning?'

'They probably went straight to Mrs. Moor at Richmond Road, saw the Jaguar, and knew there was nothing to worry about,' said Dawlish. 'Then they could safely have waited round the corner, because to get back to the West End, I'd almost certainly go to King's Road and then past the Chelsea Town Hall. They were able to follow without making it obvious. I went to that particular telephone kiosk and gave them the chance they were waiting for. So—'

Beresford rumbled, 'I get you, old chap. They may have had their orders to shoot if you called on Hardy or Moor. In other words, you weren't to live to tell anyone that men as well as the pretties were missing. Right?'

'It couldn't be more right.'

'Why *are* they missing?' Beresford asked, owlishly.

Beresford left when it was quite dark outside, promising to find out what he could of the love-life betweeen Mrs. Lorne and the missing men.

Dawlish studied the names and addresses and the pictures of the girls, then made notes of what had happened since Trivett had come to see him at the club.

It was nearly six o'clock when he heard footsteps of at least two women in the mews. He listened casually, and heard them coming up the steps. He was at the door before they rang the bell.

Felicity was standing with a younger woman, who looked pretty and charming in the light which fell on her face. Dawlish jumped to the conclusion that her name was Hilda Green.

CHAPTER SIXTEEN

SISTER

The girl wasn't much more than twenty, and had a youthful eagerness which was attractive in itself.

Felicity closed the door.

'Pat,' she said, 'this is Millicent Green—Hilda Green's sister.'

This wasn't going according to plan, either; practically nothing went according to plan.

Millicent Green's hand-clasp was firm.

'I'm terribly worried,' she said.

Dawlish put a hand on Millicent Green's arm and ushered her into the living-room.

'Her sister is missing,' Felicity announced.

'She is, Mr. Dawlish. In fact, if I hadn't met Mrs. Dawlish, I should have gone to the police to-day. Hilda disappeared three days ago. She just went out to do some shopping, and didn't come back.'

Dawlish released her arm, went silently to the cocktail cabinet, and began to pour drinks.

At closer quarters and in the better light, Millicent Green proved to have green-grey eyes, rather like Felicity's. She was tall and had not properly filled out, but her figure held much promise. Youthful anxiety showed in the intensity of her eyes. Her complexion was superb, and her hair was light brown.

'Tell me more,' said Dawlish, humbly. 'Let me see if I can get something right.'

'Well—there isn't much more to tell you. It started when Hilda got this job with Mrs. Lorne. Hilda's two years older than I, although we look much alike, we're sometimes taken for twins. She's an expert shorthand-typist, I'm *hopeless* at anything except fiddling about with clothes. She wanted a job that was a bit out of the ordinary, and Mrs. Lorne said that she travelled a great deal, there was even a chance that this would mean a visit to South America. So Hilda jumped at it.'

Felicity looked over her shoulder, and mouthed, '*South America. White—slaves.*'

'How did she get in touch with Mrs. Lorne?' asked Dawlish, ignoring his wife.

'Through a friend, I don't know the friend's name. She knew another girl who'd worked for Mrs. Lorne, and Mrs. Lorne was advertising in the *Evening News*. That was two weeks ago. And on Monday—'

Monday was the day the various men had disappeared.

'—we went to a cocktail party. Hilda was looking forward to starting the new job, and we talked about it quite a bit. A queer thing happened. Hilda's a career-woman, if you know what I mean, and she hasn't had much time for serious *affaires*. But she's several men friends, and one of them has been pretty anxious to be really serious. I mean, marriage. He was at the party. When Hilda said she was going to work for this Mrs. Lorne, he looked as if he'd fall through the floor. It was really embarrassing. He told her that she was simply being a fool, that a professional career was folly, that she ought to marry and have children and give up this nonsense about working. That kind of thing. The odd thing was that he looked livid. There wasn't exactly a row, but Hilda let him know pretty well what she thought, and he left the party early. Next morning, Hilda went out to do some shopping and didn't come home. I thought nothing of it, but she wasn't back by tea-time. Then I had a telephone message, that she was with friends and might be away a day or two— would I send some clothes to the Red Lion Hotel, Kingston? I sent them with a friend, I had to go to a mannequin parade that night. I thought Hilda would be at the hotel, but she wasn't—the case had to be left for her to collect. I haven't had a word since. I started talking, and Mrs. Dawlish managed to make me say what was in my mind. I'd hesitated, until then. Now—'

'Miss Green was the man who made the fuss at the cocktail party a Mr. Moor? Or a Mr. Reginald Hardy?'

'How on earth did you know? It was Reggie Hardy.'

'Mr. Hardy also vanished, about the same time,' Dawlish said. 'Fel, I'm going out for an hour or two. Can you stay here, Miss Green?'

'Well, I can, but—'

'Then please do. Tell my wife everything you can about the Red Lion. If the friend who took the clothes there for you can come here and talk about what happened, it would be a help. Organise things, Fel, will you?'

'Yes. Where are you going?'

'To see Hardy's man,' said Dawlish.

He went into the hall, slid into a coat, and hurried out. For once, Felicity did not follow him to utter warning counsel. It was cold, the stars were bright, and the distant rumble of London's traffic made a constant background of sound. He went to the car, and saw a shadowy figure in a corner of the mews.

'Hello, Hennessey,' said Dawlish, as the blond sergeant's face showed. 'Did anything happen tonight?'

'I'm pretty sure your wife wasn't followed,' said Hennessey.

'Be very careful with her, won't you?'

'Are you going to be out for long?'

'Not a minute longer than I can help. If I shouldn't be around by midnight, tell Mr. Trivett that I was last known to be interrogating the manservant of Mr. Reginald Hardy, will you?'

He pulled up outside Number 27 Liddel Street and looked up at the third floor.

A light showed dimly against the curtains.

He went up the narrow stairs quickly, and paused only when he reached the front door. He didn't ring, at first; but considered possibilities. Then he rang the bell.

There was no answer.

He rang again.

He rang for the third time, with no response.

It was very quiet on the landing, and the light here was poor.

He took out a torch, examined the lock, and was satisfied that it would not be difficult to force. He opened a blade in his pen-knife, which served as a skeleton key; it was dwarfed in his hand. He moved it dexterously, and the key caught, the lock clicked back. He put the knife away and switched off the torch, then opened the door.

A light was on in the hall, also, and the doors inside the flat were open. He heard nothing. He pushed the front door to, but didn't latch it, and stepped towards the door of what looked like a living-room.

Reginald Hardy's grey-haired servant lay on the floor. His head was horribly battered, blood spattered the carpet.

Dawlish went straight to the telephone, dialled 999 and when he got through to the Information Room at Scotland Yard, asked for a squad car and an ambulance to come to Liddel Street at once; and added the magic name of Trivett. Then he turned, and heard a faint groan.

He knelt by the man's side.

His pulse was beating, and he was breathing, he even seemed to be on the verge of consciousness. Dawlish stood up and took out his hip-flask, poured a little brandy into the cap, eased the man up and gave him a sip. The man's eyes flickered once or twice.

Dawlish said: 'Listen carefully. Mr. Hardy left on Monday, and you know where he is, but had orders not to tell anyone.'

'Yes,' came a whisper.

'The men who broke in to-night made you tell them—didn't they?'

'Yes,' the man sighed.

'You know that Mr. Hardy's in danger. I think I can help him. Where is he?'

'He's at—seventeen—Willow Court—Putney.'

'Is Miss Green with him?'

'Yes, yes,' he gasped. 'Yes.'

Dawlish stood up. Minutes might matter: the police and the ambulance should be here in a few minutes. He picked up a newspaper, took out his pen and wrote across the news: '*17 Willow Court, Putney. Hurry. Murder.*' He dropped the newspaper at the man's feet, and hurried out. He heard a car approaching, and it passed him when he was at the end of the street; a Flying Squad car. A hundred yards farther along, he heard the ringing of an ambulance bell. He didn't slacken speed for either, ignored the speed limits and roared along King's Road, towards Fulham and Putney.

CHAPTER SEVENTEEN

HARDY AND FRIEND

Dawlish saw the number 17 in chromium figures on the door immediately in front of him. He didn't try to pick this lock, the time for finesse was gone. He gripped the handle, put his shoulder to the door, and exerted every ounce of his massive strength. The door creaked and groaned. He drew back, and launched himself at it; it groaned again.

At the next attempt, the door gave a final, agonised groan, and burst inwards. Dawlish was pitched forward, staggering, losing his balance. He saw a man in an open doorway; he didn't see the gun in the man's hand, but heard the report of the shot and saw the flash. The bullet went over his head. He thought he heard a gasp as he pitched forward in a headlong tackle. His hands gripped the ankles of the man with the gun; he knew that the other might point the gun downwards, that if he fired again there wasn't a chance. The danger lasted for a split second; and then he tugged and the man crashed down.

His fall shook the floor.

Dawlish looked up. A door banged somewhere else in the flat. The man he'd brought down wasn't hurt, and still held his gun. Dawlish snatched at his wrist and twisted; an anguished gasp followed, the gun dropped from nerveless fingers. Dawlish picked it up, and got to his feet.

The man he'd attacked was on the floor, holding his right wrist, his face pale with the pain. Apart from that, the flat seemed empty. Dawlish went through another door and found himself in a kitchen; the door which led to the fire-escape wasn't locked. He opened it and peered out. He heard running footsteps again; had little doubt that there had been two men, and that one had escaped.

He turned back. A man stood uncertainly in the doorway. Dawlish's victim was getting slowly to his feet; and there was an ugly look in his eyes. As Dawlish neared him, he snatched at his pocket—and Dawlish imagined either a knife or another gun. He brought his right fist up beneath the man's chin, and the blow lifted the other's feet from the floor. He fell like a dog.

The man in the doorway said, 'What the devil *is* all this?'

'Police,' said Dawlish, to save time.

Cars were drawing up outside; he felt pretty sure that the police were already downstairs. He left the man to welcome the police and tried the dining-room. He tried two more doors which opened into more empty rooms; and found a fourth, locked. He banged on it.

'Hardy! Miss Green! Are you there?'

Yard men and local police were already spilling into the flat, but they stopped at sight of Dawlish. Into the hush came a man's voice, pitched on a low note.

'Who—who's that?'

'Police. You're all right,' said Dawlish.

'Can you—can you prove it?' called the man from behind the locked door.

'Just wait a moment, sir, I'll push my card of authority under the door,' said one of the police, a uniformed sergeant with a red face. The man out of sight said:

'It's alright, darling, we're safe.'

Reginald Hardy was a man of medium height, and looked as hard as nails. His face was tanned, he hadn't an ounce of loose flesh, and he moved with the springiness of the athlete in training. He was rather pale beneath his tan, and his eyes held shadows, as if fear hadn't quite gone. Hilda Green was almost as tall as Hardy. She had fairer hair and a rounded chin, but the same green-grey eyes as Millicent. She was pale and trembling. Hardy shielded Hilda Green as from ravening wolves, although no one tried to prevent him from going into the drawing-room. He helped her into a chair, poured her out a drink, and stood over her while she sipped it.

Dawlish was talking and explaining to the sceptical sergeant and while he talked, a Scotland Yard Squad car arrived, and among the men was one whom Dawlish knew. The Putney sergeant accepted Dawlish's story for the first time—and agreed that it would be wise if the girl were left to recover from whatever ordeal she had suffered.

'Just what *has* happened?' asked the sergeant of Hardy

'Well—I had reason to believe that Miss Green—my fiancée— and I were in danger. I brought her here, I've kept this flat as a little *pied-à-terre* for some time, in case I ever wanted to hide. And—'

'Hide from whom, sir?' asked the sergeant.

'I've enemies,' Hardy said abruptly. 'I'll discuss that at Scotland Yard. They found us here and broke in, about ten minutes before you came. I heard them, bundled Hilda into the bathroom and jammed a chair under the handle. I was scared, I don't mind admitting that. They're killers.'

'You ought to know that the beggars visited your Sloane Square flat first, and that your man's badly hurt.'

'Badly? Are you sure? Where—?'

'Let's get to the Yard,' Dawlish said. 'We can find everything out from there. And we'll drop Miss Green at my flat, on the way. She'll find her sister there, and can stay the night if necessary.'

Hardy's manservant was on the danger list, but there was a fair chance of his recovery.

'Now when did it start?' asked Trivett.

'*This* particular show began when I heard from Geraldine Lorne again,' said Hardy grimly. 'I thought I'd finished with her. That woman's a devil. Better go back a bit farther, though. I met Geraldine Lorne in France, just over three years ago. Her husband had just died. She was pretty hot, if you know what I mean. I was attracted by her. Went along to her house for a little party. Er—not the kind of thing one boasts to the police about. Must have been drunk, to stand it. She was a degenerate, of course—you'll know that. Had a lot of fancy tricks to show us. Well, that's how it started. There were just half a dozen of us, and—well, this is the queer thing. By day, Geraldine Lorne was the sweetest thing you could imagine. It was as if she had two selves, and the second self only popped out now and again.'

Trivett nodded, encouragingly.

'She fascinated me. Never met a woman like her. Just couldn't tear myself away from her. Then—' He paused, and looked more uncomfortable than he had all the time. 'Then she asked me to sell some jewels for her. I had one or two friends in the jewel trade. To cut a long story short, I sold them. Sold others, later. It wasn't for the better part of a year that I discovered they were stolen. I was going to walk out, but she—well, see what a fix

I was in? Yes, she blackmailed me. Then I discovered she was mixed up in several other kinds of crime—dope, that kind of thing. I couldn't take it, and just packed up. I know, I know, I should have told the police, and might have done—but for the fact that one of the little crowd got in first. She had an answer for everything, and—the man who talked committed suicide.'

Hardy looked straight at Trivett, and there was a bleak look in his eyes. His voice hardened as he went on:

'She "proved"—no one will ever know how she fixed it—that he owed her a fortune, and was trying to get out of paying by slandering her. The whole affair was hushed up, as it often is on the Riviera, and I just walked out. I thought it was over and done with, until a few days ago. Last week, in fact. I had a telephone message, saying she wanted to see me. I was to meet her in the foyer of the Ritz. I ignored it. As it happened, a couple of days afterwards I was at a cocktail party with my fian—with Miss Green. Imagine what I thought when I heard she was going to work for Geraldine Lorne. I made a complete fool of myself. On the way home from the cocktail party, I was stopped by a couple of young fellows. They told me that Geraldine Lorne wanted to see me and told me I had to go with them. I hit one of them pretty hard, I can tell you, but instead of running off, they kept at it. Started threatening Hilda. I knew the kind of thing of which that woman was capable, and—well, I panicked. Could have gone to the police, but it would have sounded like a lot of hot-air. I didn't want the past dragged out, either. I waited for Hilda next day, met her when she was going out to do some shopping, and convinced her that Geraldine Lorne was a nasty piece of work. Told her pretty well what I've told you. She responded wonderfully. She could see the spot I was in, and— well, I found that she'd been more fond of me than I'd realised. Tonight, these men came. They'd been inside for five minutes when there was a disturbance at the door. Soon afterwards, you arrived, Dawlish. That was that.'

'How many men?' asked Dawlish, almost lazily.

'Two. One got away, didn't he?'

'Yes. Did you know any of Mrs. Lorne's other friends well?' asked Dawlish.

'Not really. We were competitors, so to speak. Only two were close personal friends. The man who died and Tommy Moor.'

Dawlish kept a blank face at mention of Moor—for he had thought a lot about the man whose house had been burgled and who had thereafter been a changed man.

'How did Moor take it?'

'He packed up almost at once, swearing vengeance. That turned him against Geraldine Lorne, of course. It was a lot of hot-air—he did nothing.'

Dawlish felt even greater interest in Thomas Moor.

CHAPTER EIGHTEEN

FLY AWAY, GERALDINE

As he drove to the flat in the mews, Hardy sat by his side, looking straight ahead of him, and didn't speak.

It was now after ten o'clock.

Lights blazed from the flat windows. Hennessey was still standing in the shadows, and didn't come forward when he saw that there was someone else with Dawlish. Felicity opened the door as Dawlish and Hardy reached the top step.

'You wouldn't remember that I haven't had dinner and didn't have much lunch, would you?' asked Dawlish plaintively.

'Must you always think about food?' asked Felicity sweetly. 'Good evening, Mr. Hardy.'

'Oh, yes. Hardy, my wife.' He gave a slow smile, and Hardy glanced at him as if puzzled at the change in him; this man looked incapable of sudden, violent action and of making swift decisions.

It was so arranged that Millicent Green and Felicity spent the next quarter of an hour in the kitchen, that Dawlish had a shower, and Hardy and Hilda Green were together in the living-room. When Dawlish went in, heralding his arrival with a loud cough, Hardy got up quickly from the arm of the girl's chair.

'Oh, Dawlish,' Hardy said, rather too abruptly. 'In the rush, we completely forgot to say—well, to say thanks.'

Dawlish waved his hand.

'Please, no! There's one thing, though. Why? I mean, why should they be so determined to kill you?'

'I've told you everything I know. I've kept a lot hidden, but I've sense enough to see that it had to come out now. Possibly Geraldine Lorne thinks I can give her away. It wouldn't surprise me of you don't find a lot of criminal history when you start to dig into her past.'

'Ever meet a chap named Kane? Sebastian Kane?'

'Yes, quite often. He was Geraldine Lorne's chief dupe. You might almost call him a lackey, he'd run errands, do anything for her. He worshipped her. He'd turn up at odd times, unexpectedly, and follow her about like a dog. In a way,' said Hardy, choosing his words carefully, 'it was pathetic. But if you liked to look at it another way, it was revolting!'

'When did you last see Kane?'

'It must have been eighteen months or so ago. The last time I went to the Riviera. I was only there a few days, had the row, and left.'

'Sure there were only two men at your flat to-night?'

'I only heard two,' Hardy said, eyeing Dawlish intently. 'I certainly didn't seen Kane, if that's what you're getting at. If he were there, I think I should have known. He could never keep quiet, even when he whispered it was like a bull-frog croaking. He's just naturally noisy and clumsy. You can take it that Kane wasn't there to-night.'

Felicity came in with a laden trolley.

'Oh, well,' said Dawlish, almost sadly, and then he studied the food and his eyes brightened. 'This doesn't look too bad. We've something to celebrate, too. We mustn't be too late, though.

Hilda has to start her new job in the morning.' He beamed at the girl, ignoring her astonished look.

Hardy spoke first, and hesitantly.

'You can't be serious, Dawlish. I wouldn't let Hilda go anywhere near the woman.'

'I hope you will,' said Dawlish. 'It should be an interesting first session.'

'Do you think it will help you?' Hilda Green asked quietly.

'Great Scott, yes. You'll be forewarned, you'll be watched carefully by the police, there isn't anything really dangerous in it. If Geraldine doesn't know that you've plighted your troth, you might discover many things to help clear up the mystery.'

He talked, at some length, after supper.

Geraldine Lorne opened the door of the flat herself, and her face lit up when she saw Hilda. She held out a welcoming hand, and drew the girl into the flat. As the door closed, they seemed shut off from the rest of London—perhaps from security. Geraldine's eyes were bright and her manner warm, as they went across to the drawing-room. Yet there was a hint of shadow on her face.

'Hilda—we're going to call each other by our Christian names, I can't stand formality—I hope we're going to get along well. And thank goodness *someone* has turned up, I'm in a hopeless mess. You won't believe it, looking at me, but I've a dreadful headache this morning. I'm going to lie down for half an hour. Just—just carry on.'

Geraldine waved her hand vaguely about the room, and went out.

As her bedroom door closed, Hilda Green smiled delightedly.

* * *

Trivett entered the mews first, about half-past ten next morning, and found Dawlish lying back in the largest easy-chair, legs stretched straight out, pipe dropping on to his chest, eyes half-closed. Without preamble he said:

'There's no trace of any of the missing girls, none of Thomas Moor or the other missing men. Geraldine Lorne hasn't been out of her flat since she turned up again—at least, she hasn't been out of the building. That's *quite* certain. Kane's been there once or twice, but spends most of his time at his own flat, and he hasn't had any visitors.'

Dawlish contemplated the wisdom of telling Trivett about Loretta Mannion now; and rejected it.

'The prisoners all stick to the same story. They were hired by a man they don't know, paid a hundred pounds in pound notes each, and told exactly what to do. The first brace were to kill you; the second, to kill Reginald Hardy.'

'Couldn't be Kane?'

'The man was a stranger, but certainly not Kane. One good thing's come of it. We've raided a couple of clubs, one in Soho and one in Limehouse, taken a dozen men who had guns and ammunition without a licence.'

'Why the visit?' asked Dawlish.

'I've a report on Geraldine Lorne, from France. This man Hardy says committed suicide was killed; suicide was the official explanation. He did make charges which weren't substantiated. The Riviera police weren't satisfied, but Geraldine Lorne left the district soon afterwards, and they were quite happy to be rid of her. There was a lot of burglary around that time—big, spectacular robbery, too. The police thought it was organised, but much of it stopped after Mrs. Lorne left the Riviera. There was plenty of gold smuggling and some drug trafficking—there usually is, out there. They can't say that the currency smuggling eased much, as far as they know; drug traffic certainly slackened.'

'You knew that Hilda Green took up her post, didn't you?'

'Yes, you told me. I've detailed men, to look after her.'

'There's another thing of interest, Bill. A couple I've known for years, man and wife, the man butler and wife cook-general, have taken the job with Geraldine. Middle-aged, tough, and they know the risks. Geraldine has three members of the household who will pass on everything of interest. Kane's been to see her once or twice. Hilda Green says that she thinks that beneath her gaiety, Geraldine is scared stiff. She's sure Kane is. I've kept away from each of them, just to let the yeast of anxiety ferment nicely. We're going to have a blow up soon, and it'll be a big one. I'll make two guesses. That Reginald Hardy will be attacked again, pretty soon—that's why he's staying at this flat. And that there'll be more funny business with the person of Geraldine. Have you checked the other flats in Hailey Court?'

'I've no information suggesting that she knows anyone else at the flats, or could go to anyone else when in trouble.'

'Where is Hardy now?'

'He's gone to see his man in hospital,' Dawlish grinned. 'He knows there's danger, but has decided to square his shoulders and face the enemy.'

Trivett said thoughtfully, 'Did you take his story at its face value?'

'I'm inclined to believe him.'

As he broke off, the telephone bell rang. He stretched out his hand for it, lazily.

'Dawlish speaking.'

He heard what might have been a gasp, then an urgent, frightened voice:

'Mr. Dawlish, this is Hilda Green. Kane's *killing* Reggie.'

CHAPTER NINETEEN

FREE FIGHT

The lift shot up.

'How long have you known about the shindy?' asked Dawlish of the commissionaire at Hailey Court.

'It was first reported by the lady in the next flat, there was a lot of shouting and some screaming. Ten minutes ago, I suppose, sir. We tried reasoning, but no one will listen. We're afraid—'

The lift jolted to a stop, which proved the commissionaire's frame of mind.

A man stood outside the door of Number 31, wielding an axe. Others stood watching tensely. Between the rending noises of the axe smashing into the thick wood, came other sounds—thudding and shouting. As Dawlish and Trivett reached the little crowd, the door shook, from something thrown at it from inside. Dawlish said:

'Let me have a go.'

The work was nearly done. Two heavy blows with the axe and the door yielded a couple of inches. Something else thudded against it, from the inside. Dawlish put his weight to it.

A chair was blocking the door. Dawlish pushed his hand

through the opening, felt for the chair and managed to push it away from the handle. Then the door swung open. He stepped inside, his right hand at his pocket.

Hardy stood on the far side of the room, collar and coat torn, hair falling into his eyes, teeth bared, gasping for breath. He held a small chair, and flung it as Dawlish sidled inside. Kane, alongside the wall nearer Dawlish ducked to avoid it, and it smashed against the wall. Kane gave a bull-like bellow and rushed forward as Hardy grabbed a small table—much lighter than the chair, the only remaining weapon in sight.

Kane's hair was hanging over his forehead, his coat was ripped at one shoulder, his lips were turned back, and his eyes were blood-shot like the eyes of a rogue elephant. The other doors leading from the hall were closed, except those leading into the bathroom and the kitchen; broken crockery lay on the floor of the kitchen, a smashed chair reeled against the enamel-topped table.

Kane jumped forward.

Hardy smashed the table at his head, but the giant brushed it aside with one arm. Hardy, near a corner, shot out his right foot; he'd some practice in unarmed combat. It rammed Kane in the stomach, and the big man dropped back, grunting; he looked more wild than before.

Neither man appeared to have noticed Dawlish or the others who streamed in.

'Peace,' said Dawlish, in a deep voice.

Hardy didn't look away from Kane, but Kane darted a swift, startled glance towards Dawlish, who went in, with both fists. Kane was already near exhaustion, and hardly put up a fight. A right to the jaw sent him against the wall, and he staggered along it, hands in front of his face, the savagery beginning to fade. Two men from outside took their lives in their hands and ranged alongside him.

His breathing sounded like hissing steam.

Hardy brushed his hair out of his eyes, and stood with his feet wide apart and his hands limp by his side; near exhaustion.

'All right, Hilda,' Dawlish said clearly. 'The fight's over. Is Mrs. Lorne with you?'

'No, she's out. Reggie locked the door, please open it.'

The key was in the outside of the door. The girl came out slowly, pale to the lips, her eyes heavy with dread. She saw Hardy, gave a little cry, and ran towards him. He looked as if he might collapse. She put an arm round his waist and helped him out of the hall into the drawing-room.

She helped Hardy to sit down. His knuckles were bleeding, and there was a cut on his chin, but otherwise he showed no injuries. A scratch on Kane's cheek had bled freely, and made him look a wild, animal figure.

A Yard man, who had been on duty outside, came hurrying into the room. Trivett dealt briefly and pleasantly with the other people, shepherded them out and left Kane standing against the wall, with only the Yard man watching over him. Trivett closed the smashed door, as nearly as he could; but anything said in the hall would be heard outside.

Kane drew in a deep, rasping breath.

'What started the fight?' Trivett asked abruptly.

'Hardy came here and wanted to see Geraldine. She had the luck this time, I was in and she was out.'

'And you just lammed into him,' said Dawlish.

'He took a poke at me,' Kane said.

'Sure.'

'Even little starry-eyes will tell you that,' sneered Kane.

Hilda Green was too busy looking after Hardy to hear that, but when Hardy was sitting back in an easy-chair, a patch of sticking-plaster over the cut on his chin, she told her story.

Geraldine Lorne had gone out only five minutes before Hardy had called. Kane had opened the door. They'd started to quarrel, and Hardy had pushed his way in; that had led to the first blow.

'You'd better come away, Mr. Hardy,' said Trivett.

'And you can take starry-eyes with you,' sneered Kane. 'We don't want any of Dawlish's spies hanging around the flat. The couple went out on their ear after breakfast. I discovered they'd come from you, too. Clear out, Dawlish. I can handle Mrs. Lorne's affairs.'

'I don't know,' said Dawlish. 'I'll wait until I've seen Mrs. Lorne.'

The words were calculated to test Kane's mood; and Kane growled a protest, but didn't start to throw his weight about. Trivett took statements from all three, and Hardy's gave a simple explanation: he had gone to 'have it out' with Geraldine, after seeing his man and realising how badly Pendle had been hurt.

Hardy and Hilda left half an hour afterwards, and Trivett waited only to speak to Dawlish.

'Be careful,' he said. 'Kane doesn't like you.'

Kane and Dawlish, in the drawing-room, sat glaring at each other.

Dawlish said mildly: 'What really started it?'

Kane said: 'You did. When I discovered you'd sent that couple, I made a few inquiries. I discovered that Hardy was staying with you, and Hardy's no friend of Geraldine's.'

Dawlish mused: 'Suggesting that Hardy's one of the people Geraldine's scared of?'

'It wouldn't surprise me. He's a swine.'

'Where is she?'

'*I* don't know.'

* * *

Dawlish did not go straight to the mews, but, as if drawn by factors he couldn't understand, went to see Mrs. Moor at Chelsea. She had recollected nothing more, but was sure that from the night of the burglary, her husband had been a different man.

Hardy and Hilda were at the mews flat when Dawlish arrived, a little before one o'clock. Her sister and Felicity were out, only the daily woman was in the flat with them. Hardy said abruptly:

'Sorry, Dawlish. I simply went to see Geraldine, to find out if I could scare her. Didn't expect I'd bump into Kane. He just went wild. I'm afraid something might happen to Hilda. I wasn't happy about her taking up the position. It preyed on my mind.'

Dawlish grinned.

'Any man of your size who can stand up to Kane for a quarter of an hour has everything it takes.'

'I've boxed a bit,' Hardy said, casually. 'Commando trained, too. Mind you, he's as powerful as an ox, I don't like to think what would have happened if you hadn't turned up when you did. Well, at least Hilda's away—it was worth it, if only for that. I know you probably think I'm crazy, but Kane *did* find out about the servants.'

'What about Kane's broad hint that you've caused Geraldine a lot of bother?'

'I've told you everything I know, Dawlish. Kane was lying.'

'When did you last see Geraldine?'

'Eighteen months ago.'

'She hasn't shown up personally, of late?'

'No. I didn't even know she was in London, until she phoned me last week. For all I knew, she was still in the South of France. Well, that's it and all there is about it, Dawlish. I'll do anything I can to help, but I don't think there's any point, in staying here any longer. Hilda and Millicent can go back to their flat, I'll go to Sloane Square—and if you've time on Tuesday, you might be a witness at our wedding. Yes, I've fixed a special licence!'

'The latest problem of real interest,' said Dawlish, as he lay back in the arm-chair, late that evening, 'is why Reginald Hardy is so anxious to get married in such a hurry. Yes, it could be young love, or—'

He shrugged his shoulders. He had made exhaustive inquiries, and discovered nothing fresh. It was a simple fact that all of Geraldine Lorne's close acquaintances had disappeared. Trivett had found no one else who claimed to know her. The French police were trying to trace some of the Frenchmen who had been among her small circle of close friends on the Riviera; no reports were yet through.

'Well, Geraldine Lorne hasn't been seen since she left the flat and vanished,' Felicity said. 'Remember that? The only contact you have now, darling, is Kane, and he's just taken possession of 31 Hailey Court, and says he won't leave until she comes back.'

Felicity sounded very matter-of-fact.

'Dull life, isn't it?' asked Dawlish.

Felicity spoke again, but with a little less assurance.

'All you can do, Pat, is sit there puffing away at your pipe and looking like a stuffed owl. There isn't anything else you *can* do. No one's going to start attacking you again, if you withdraw. *I* don't want to be a widow. It would be different if you knew who was behind it, or if you had any real clue as to what's happening, but you haven't. It frightens me. It's crazy to go on, knowing—'

'Practically the whole story,' Dawlish said blandly.

CHAPTER TWENTY

HUMBLE KANE

Ted Beresford did not raise an eyebrow, but took his pipe from his lips and said sonorously:

'I don't believe a word of it.'

'Of course you don't know the whole story.' Felicity was almost angry.

'A prophet has no honour in his own country,' said Dawlish sadly. 'Very soon, I'm going to have another chat with Kane. If things go well after the explosion, he'll come to the end of his tether and be willing to accept help. Then he'll probably—'

'*Kane* won't let *you* help now,' Felicity declared.

'Most unlikely,' said Beresford.

Knowing that he was being irritating, Dawlish gave a superior grin, but before he could speak again, the telephone bell rang. As it rang, the front-door bell burred. Dawlish stretched out his hand for the telephone.

'Dawlish speaking,' said Dawlish into the telephone.

'Hallo, Pat.' It was Trivett. 'I thought you'd like to know that—'

He broke off, and Dawlish heard someone speak to him. At the same time, Felicity and Beresford reached the front door and opened it; and a voice which could belong to only one man in the world sounded like a foghorn through the flat.

'Is Dawlish in?'

'Sorry,' Trivett said into the telephone. 'I was going to say, I thought you'd like to know that we've found one of the missing girls.'

Dawlish stiffened. Beresford appeared in the doorway, and Kane was peering over his shoulder. Dawlish waved them away, with his free hand. Beresford succeeded in shifting Kane backwards, and closed the door.

'Which one?'

'Loretta Mannion. Dead.'

Just for a wild moment he had thought that someone had been playing a trick which had no normal explanation.

'Where did you find her?' asked Dawlish.

'In the river, just north of Kingston-on-Thames.' Trivett was almost brusque. 'She'd been strangled, and dead for two or three days. The body was naked, but there'd been no attempt to disfigure the face. The size of the bruises, as far as we can judge, are identical with those on Tim's throat, and on Rumbold's—it was manual strangulation by someone with very big hands.'

Outside, Kane was protesting vigorously and noisily.

'We haven't found a trace of any of the others, nor of Geraldine Lorne,' Trivett went on. 'I've just come from a session with the Assistant Commissioner. We've decided that we can't be fobbed off by Kane any longer. We're going to regard Mrs. Lorne as missing, and put out a general call for her. We're going to give her picture to the newspapers, and—'

'I shouldn't,' Dawlish said. 'Not yet.'

'I must.'

'Well, you're the boss. Anything else?'

'We've nothing on Kane. We don't know when Loretta

Mannion was murdered, so we can't say whether he had an opportunity or not. We're still unable to find out where he was when Tim and Rumbold were attacked We've managed to get measurements of his hands and fingers, and there's no doubt that he's got the right-sized hands. So—'

'You're not going to hold *him*?' Dawlish sounded alarmed.

'We're going to pull him in for questioning about Geraldine Lorne and Loretta Mannion,' said Trivett. 'Judging from the way he's been behaving, he'll give away under questioning. You've had a long run, Pat, we can't do anything else now.'

'*I've* had a long run.' Dawlish barked the words. 'Oh, all right. When does this start?'

'The Press will have the story in the morning. We'll wait until Kane's had a chance to see the newspapers, and then tackle him,' said Trivett.

'Low cunning and psychological pressure,' remarked Dawlish, and forced his voice to be calm. 'All right, Bill. Thanks for telling me.'

He rang off, and Kane raised his voice outside and said something about getting in to see Dawlish if he had to break the door down. Dawlish went across to the door, and pulled it open suddenly. Beresford had his back to it, Kane was staring at him threateningly.

Kane glowered: 'I thought you were trying to stall.'

'I was busy. But I'm not dying to see you, if that's what you mean.' Dawlish smiled, nastily. 'The last time we met, you were going to rub me off the face of the earth if I didn't keep my ugly nose out of this business. Remember?'

'Yes, I know,' said Kane. He bit his lips. 'Can't help it, Dawlish. I'm not—not myself. I'm living in hell.' He came forward, and Dawlish, with an eye for these things, saw that Felicity looked at the giant almost with compassion; Beresford was simply curious. 'I—I need your help, Dawlish. I can't stand the strain any longer. Geraldine asked me to promise to say nothing if she didn't show up for a few days. She's terrified of the police.' He flung that out almost defiantly, although he was doing his best to sound humble. 'You're the only man who might help to find her, apart from the police. I know there's a risk you'll go running to them, after this, but I had to take it.' He pressed a hand against his forehead, as if his head were torturing him. 'Will you help?'

'Why is Geraldine so frightened of the police?'

'I don't know. All I know is, she's done nothing to be ashamed of. Nothing!'

Dawlish thought Kane knew; felt sure that he was lying. Beresford shook his head slightly, as if to convey the opinion that Kane's word wasn't worth the breath used up to utter it. Felicity—and Felicity was a keen judge of people—kept staring at the big explorer as if she were trying to pierce his façade and see the real man.

'Will you help?' repeated Kane hoarsely. 'Damn it, if you want me to eat humble pie, *I* don't mind. I've acted like a fool. I apologise. I wouldn't have talked or acted the way I have if I hadn't been so worried. *Will* you help?'

Felicity gave an almost imperceptible nod.

'Yes,' said Dawlish.

Kane's eyes glowered, he shot out his right hand and gripped Dawlish's; the sudden pressure was so great that it almost made Dawlish wince. He pumped Dawlish's arm up and down vigorously and looked perilously as if he were going to slap him on the back.

'That's wonderful!' Kane boomed. 'In spite of all the nonsense I've talked, I've a great opinion of you, Dawlish. I know you're good. I make a hash of everything I attempt—look at the way I tried to beat Hardy up. You—'

'Incidentally, why *did* you beat Hardy up?'

'I've told you. That man's a snake, and Geraldine hated the sight of him. But you're too wide to be fooled by Reginald Hardy!' Kane brushed that aside as if it weren't worth considering, took Dawlish's arm and drew nearer, as if to breathe some gargantuan confidence into his ear; the whisper would almost certainly have reached any room in the flat. 'There's just one clue. There's a little woman who worked for Geraldine some years ago, lives at Clapham. I *think* she might know where Geraldine is.'

'Have you asked her?'

'Oh, yes,' said Kane, and gave a shamefaced grin. 'Went over there this morning, and had a look round. She didn't like it, but she couldn't very well stop me. Geraldine certainly isn't in her house, but I'm pretty sure she could tell us a thing or two. The thing is, Dawlish, Geraldine thinks the wise thing is to hide, but *I'm* not sure. And there's always the nagging fear that she might not be hiding, but that she's been kidnapped. You'll soon get the truth out of Annie.'

'Annie?'

'Annie Mellor, this old girl.'

'Where does she live?'

'Just near Clapham Common. I forget the name of the street, but I can take you there,' said Kane eagerly. 'Will you come right away?'

'But it's nearly ten o'clock,' said Felicity. 'Surely it can wait until the morning.'

Kane gaped. He didn't speak but bent upon Felicity a look of such reproach that she wilted. Beresford grinned; any man who could make Felicity wilt earned his admiration. Dawlish chuckled.

'Give me ten minutes, old chap.'

'Wonderful!' roared Kane. 'Sure, I'll give you ten minutes. My car's outside, we'll be there in no time. Dawlish, you've given me the first breath of real hope I've had since Geraldine went. I don't mind admitting I'm in love with her.'

'No!' breathed Beresford.

'Oh, but I am,' said Kane earnestly. 'And if you knew her as well as I do, you'd understand.'

'I'm sure he would,' Dawlish said, straight-faced. 'Ted, give Kane a drink, will you? I'll be back in a couple of jiffs. Whisky for me.'

He went towards the door and drew Felicity with him. Kane beamed after him, fatuously; and was still beaming when Dawlish closed the door and placed his hand over Felicity's mouth. She gurgled protestingly.

He took his hand away.

'That meant, say nothing within earshot, explorers often have big ears,' said Dawlish, and led her into the bedroom.

There, he kissed her, and she freed herself and looked at him, half-laughing, half-questioning.

'That kiss was for falling for Seb Kane's new line,' said Dawlish.

'New line? I feel sorry for the big ape. Are you trying to tell me that you think he's lying?'

'About something, yes. We'll reserve judgment. I'll go in his car. I'd like Ted to follow in his, and you to follow Ted in the Jaguar. I'll hold him up in Piccadilly so that you can catch us up, and he won't know that it's you behind. Oh—and slip out, now, to a telephone, will you? Call Trivett, if he isn't there his deputy, and ask for Kane's car to be watched and its movements reported back to the Yard.'

'But if you're going to Clapham—'

'Oh, yes, so we are. Kane says we're going to sweet Annie Mellor, who lives at Clapham, doesn't he? He could even be telling the truth, although I think the sudden appearance of an old servant of Geraldine's proves he's lying. With Ted, you, and the police all on the look-out, there shouldn't be much danger of missing anything, should there? Pop out and telephone, and then come back and tell Kane how much you hope that Annie can show the way to sweet Geraldine,' said Dawlish. He kissed her lightly on the forehead and gave her a gentle push towards the door, but she didn't go immediately. She stood looking at him with a bewildered frown, started to speak, then stopped herself and turned and hurried out of the flat.

She was back when Kane drained his glass; and a slight nod told Dawlish that she had talked to the Yard.

CHAPTER TWENTY-ONE

ANNIE

Kane had a powerful Rolls-Royce, a convertible coupé. It was parked just outside the mews, and as he approached it, with Dawlish, a man who might have been Detective Sergeant Hennessey moved away. Kane appeared not to notice the man, but opened Dawlish's door for him, said: 'Mind your hands,' and closed the door with as great a care as he could have shown for Geraldine Lorne. Dawlish sat, meek and mute. Kane took the wheel, and the engine purred. The car turned into Piccadilly, and was held up at some traffic lights. It was the first in a stream of cars. As they turned green and the car moved off again, Dawlish slid his hand into his pocket. He withdrew it and tried another; then slapped his sides.

'Lost something?' asked Kane.

'Er—no. Well, not yet.' Dawlish felt and slapped vigorously, and Kane slowed down a little. 'Funny thing, I could have sworn I changed them over when I changed my bags. Keys.'

'Oh,' said Kane. 'Door keys? Don't want to go back, do you, we'll—'

'May be late,' mumbled Dawlish. 'My wife's been sleeping

badly lately, I don't want to disturb her in the early hours if I can help it. She might get nightmares. Pull up a minute, I'll have a good look.'

Kane pulled towards the kerb obediently, but was beginning to breath heavily, as if in protest. Dawlish got out of the car, shook himself, and went through each of his pockets in turn—until he saw Beresford's car, not far away. He gave a triumphant. 'Got 'em!' and climbed back into the car.

Kane went faster, handling the car with consummate ease. He didn't speak again, except to curse traffic lights whenever he couldn't beat them. He didn't appear to notice Beresford's Allard or the Jaguar, both of which followed at a discreet distance.

He may or may not have forgotten the name of the road in which he said 'Annie Mellor' lived; he certainly knew exactly where to find it, for he swung round a corner and spurted along a wide street of terraced houses, which led off the common. He pulled up smoothly half-way along, outside a house with a lamp immediately opposite the front door; the door was painted cream, and so showed up clearly in the darkness.

Two cars passed the end of the street.

On the way, police patrol cars had doubtless noted the Rolls's passing; before long its arrival here would be reported to the Information Room and a Squad car would be prowling near, to meet any emergency.

'Here we are?' Kane said superfluously, as he jumped out and then ran to open Dawlish's door. He actually helped Dawlish out. 'Now, listen, old boy. She's a stubborn old soul—quite nice, used to work for Geraldine's parents years ago. But she knows something. I'd better not come in, or she'll try to slam the door in our faces, after this morning she hasn't much time for me. Never has had, for that matter, she didn't approve of—er—of Geraldine and me.'

Dawlish found himself almost convinced that there was someone named Annie Mellor, and wondered if his earlier guessing were wide of the mark.

Kane was exuberant.

'All you want to know is if she can tell you where to find Geraldine. Er—if you slide in a crack at me, it'll probably help. Anyone who doesn't like me is a friend of Annie's.'

There were two steps leading from the pavement to the front door of the house, which was Number 33. Dawlish hadn't seen the name of the street. The houses here were all tall and narrow, with at least three storeys. There was only one bell, nothing to suggest that the place had been turned into flats. Did 'Annie' live here alone?

He slid his right hand into his pocket, and the cold steel of the gun was comforting. He pressed the bell. The engine of the Rolls-Royce purred, and he wondered if Kane were showing his hand too soon, and slipping away; but Kane only backed out of sight of the door, and then stopped. Silence fell brooding over the night, and was broken after a few seconds by footsteps which shuffled along the passage of the house.

Chains rattled, bolts were pulled; he hadn't expected that. By now, he was fully prepared to believe that Kane had told the truth, at least about Annie. If he had, most of Dawlish's theories would fall about his ears.

The door opened an inch, and a querulous voice sounded.

'Who is it? What do you mean, coming and disturbing me late at night like this? Who is it?'

'My name is Dawlish. I—'

'Never heard of you!' The querulous voice rose to a pitch of indignation. 'If there's anything you want to see me about, come in the morning. Not before ten, I'm never up before ten.'

'It's urgent,' Dawlish said, and found it difficult to be

convincing, for this was surely Miss Annie Mellor, and so Kane had not lied. 'It's about Mrs. Geraldine Lorne, who—'

'Geraldine?' The voice sharpened still further, the door opened another two inches, and the street light shone on an elderly woman with grey hair drawn back from her forehead, sharp, pinched features, dark suspicious eyes.

'Who are you—why! You devil, I told you never to set foot in this house again!'

She slammed the door—on Dawlish's foot. It recoiled against her, she gasped, and as she backed away, Dawlish stepped inside. She hadn't put on a hall light; and he felt quite sure that she had mistaken him for Kane.

'It is really urgent,' he said, looking along the hall. He saw the light switch, stretched out, and pressed it down.

The woman stood looking at him angrily, but the anger faded—as if she had mistaken him for someone else.

'And I haven't been here before,' said Dawlish.

'I can see, can't I?' complained the woman. 'You say your name is Dawlish?'

'That's right.'

'Well, if it's about Geraldine, you'd better come in,' said Annie Mellor. 'That child will be the death of me, she was always a little minx. What do you want to know about her?' She led the way along the wide passage to a door on the right; light shone from it. She pushed the door wider open and stood aside for him to pass. As he went in, his left hand closed about the gun; but the room was empty, a large room cluttered with old-fashioned furniture, the walls crammed with prints and portraits, antima-cassars on the saddle-back chairs. It was like stepping back fifty years. The electric light was shaded by tasselled silk, and cast a pink glow over the room, over the woman, and over Dawlish.

Annie Mellor wore a black dress and a knot of black beads

which fell over a flat bosom to her waist, and rattled a little as she moved. She wasn't more than five feet six in height, and in this light, looked no older than the early sixties, although her voice was that of an old woman.

'Now, what is it?'

Dawlish said apologetically: 'I wouldn't have called if it weren't urgent. I've been trying to find Mrs. Lorne for some time. I've a message for her, and it's extremely important. I've looked everywhere, and this—'

'Did that big *beast* tell you about me?'

'You mean Sebastian Kane? He—'

'I mean, that big *beast*.'

'I wheedled your name out of him,' said Dawlish uneasily. 'He thinks he's clever, but in fact he's a fool. Miss Mellor—'

'Don't you under-rate the brute,' warned Annie Mellor. 'He may be a fool, but he's a crafty fool. Dawlish, Dawlish? *I've* never heard of a Mr. Dawlish, Geraldine's never spoken of you.'

'But she and I know each other.'

The woman didn't speak, but went across to the fire-place, where logs blazed. For the first time, Dawlish saw a kettle on the hob, steaming gently, and a tea-tray on the floor by the fender. There was only one cup.

'I wonder if you do,' said Annie Mellor. 'She's never mentioned you.' The repetition fitted in with her voice, not with her appearance; she didn't seem old enough to talk like this, that was the one false note. 'I'm just going to have a cup of tea. Join me? 'I'll get another cup,' she said, and Dawlish thought that she would go out of the room—but she took a cup and saucer from a small cupboard behind the chair which was drawn up to the fire. 'As you're here, you may as well sit down,' she added ungraciously, and made the tea while he forced himself to be patient. He felt more sure than ever that Kane had told part of the truth—that

Kane believed this woman could tell him where Geraldine Lorne was.

'How long have you known her?' she asked abruptly.

'Only a few days, but—'

'Before the trouble?'

'Do you know about the trouble,' said Dawlish.

'*I'm* not a fool,' said Annie Mellor, 'and Geraldine never keeps anything from me. She thinks she does, but I always worm it out of her. I know about the trouble all right.' Annie poured tea; her hand was steady, but there were big blue veins on the back of it, and it was mottled like the hand of someone very old. 'Tell me, Mr. Dawlish, *why* do you want to find her?'

'I want to help her.'

'That's easy to say.' She held out tea. '*Very* easy to say, but I'm not sure that I believe it.'

'It's true. Thanks.'

'Sugar?'

'No, thanks.' The tea already had milk in it. 'How much do you know, Miss Mellor?'

'Plenty,' she said, and cackled, as if triumphantly. 'Geraldine's lived a fast life, she's a hussy, I've always told her that she'd regret her folly, and she's regretting it now. She's frightened, young man. Terrified. Do you know why? Because all her friends have disappeared. All the people she knew, the people she could rely on, have vanished. She's afraid of being kidnapped herself, and so she's run away, and I'm not going to tell anyone where to find her, you needn't think I am.' She sipped her tea, and looked up at him through the faint haze of steam. 'That is, unless I think they can help her.'

'I'm sure I can help,' said Dawlish.

She cackled again.

'So was that brute Kane, but I don't trust him. I'm not sure that I trust you, either. I don't know why you should be interested in Geraldine. Why *are* you?'

'I'm a friend of one of her missing friends.'

She looked as if she hadn't expected that answer, and her eyes seemed to lose something of their suspicion. The sharp features gave an indication that she had once been a handsome woman; the firm chin suggested that she could be stubborn and loyal. 'Who? Which one?'

'Thomas Moor,' said Dawlish.

'*Are* you, then,' said Annie Mellor, and sipped again. 'Well, that *is* remarkable. I always liked Thomas, although he wasn't the man for my Geraldine, *no* man will ever be good enough for her, and don't you make any mistake about it. Fancy you knowing Tommy Moor?' She cackled. 'Geraldine *will* be surprised, I'm sure. When she knows, that is. Is that the only reason why you're interested?'

'Isn't it enough?'

'No,' said Annie, bluntly. 'No, it isn't. I *might* be able to tell you where you can find Geraldine, she added cunningly, 'but first I'd have to know a lot more about you and what you're doing and all that kind of thing. I'm not a fool, young man, even if I am over seventy. Are you a policeman?' she added abruptly, and her eyes peered into his as if she were going to judge his answer from his reaction and not from anything he said.

'I am not!'

'Beware of the man who protests too much,' said Annie Mellor. She put down her cup and held her hand out for Dawlish's. 'More tea?'

'I've not quite finished.'

'Well, drink up, drink up,' she said testily. 'It's not the right stuff for you, I suppose, you'd prefer to be drinking whisky.'

She grinned as Dawlish finished his tea.

That struck another false note.

He couldn't tell why, but he didn't like the way she grinned; it was quite different from any expression she had shown so far. She had behaved more or less according to type; an old family servant who was in a secret and who relished her share in it. She was exactly what Kane had led him to expect, and that had been a blow, because he had wanted to prove that Kane had lied. He had alarmed Felicity and brought the police because he had thought that he might come to the house and find not Annie Mellor, but men of violence. The theory he had so carefully built up was toppling—but the old woman's grin steadied it.

Why?

He said slowly, 'Miss Mellor, this isn't a joking matter, and it's urgent. I have to see Mrs. Lorne. She's in considerable danger. The police are looking for her, and she needs to know that. She may find herself suspected of—'

'Well?' Annie Mellor barked. 'Suspected of what?'

'Murder,' said Dawlish.

'Don't be ridiculous, young man!'

He didn't answer. He couldn't forget that grin, although she had changed again and was talking in character, as she leaned back in that chair. She looked older than she had when she had first come into the room. Was he crazy to have any suspicions about her?

'Murder!' she snorted.

'You see,' said Dawlish, 'one of the missing friends is dead. It was murder. The police think that Mrs. Lorne probably knows something about these disappearances. They know all about them. I'm not convinced that she does, although there's a lot of evidence. If I can see her and she'll talk freely to me, she may be able to save herself.'

He stopped talking. A muzziness came over him. Then the

woman got up, brushed against him—and he felt the prick of a needle.

He tried to get up, but his strength had gone. He tried to speak, but couldn't. She had sat down again now, and there was no mistaking the grin.

It was a gloating grin, hinting of triumph, mystifying him but undoubtedly there. The prick of a needle? He sat very still, trying to impress her, but now had the feeling that she was laughing at him. He felt numbness creeping over him, as if his disappointment were making him physically tired.

'*You* can't help Geraldine to save herself,' said Annie Mellor, and looked towards the door.

That startled him, and he began to turn his head.

He couldn't.

He simply could not turn his head.

She said, 'It's all right now, Sam.'

Dawlish heard the door open, but still couldn't look round, and that realisation sent panic shooting through him. There was something the matter with the muscles of his neck. He raised his right arm, to twist his body; but his arm moved only an inch from the chair, then flopped down. Panic bit at him like angry flames, as someone came into the room. The old woman sat grinning at 'Sam', and Dawlish saw the man who appeared, a short, stocky, youngish man, who was also grinning. He was nearly bald; that made him look older than he was. He had a big chin, and walked with a swagger, stood by the woman's chair and looked down at Dawlish, who fought against the rush of fear and the horrifying realisation that he couldn't move.

'So we've got the great Dawlish,' said Sam.

'Easy, wasn't it? Just a cup of tea, with a drug added!' Annie Mellor cackled. 'Then a nice little jab with the needle. I knew we'd get him. Just as I knew Kane would do what we told him, if we used the right methods. Just make him think his Geraldine's in danger, and he'll do exactly what you want.'

Dawlish heard every word, saw every movement of her lips and the grin on the man's face. He tried to move his right hand again, but couldn't—this time, he wasn't able to lift it off the arm of the chair. He exerted himself to move in the chair, but couldn't shift an inch. It was as if some unseen vice were gripping him, paralysing his nervous system. His mind was as clear as ever it had been—the fact that he'd been fooled wasn't important; the fact that he couldn't move was desperately important.

The man named Sam moved forward, and hit him on the nose. It wasn't a hard blow, but nicely timed; and it hurt. Yet Dawlish couldn't draw his head back, could do nothing to try to dodge the blow; just had to take it. The man slapped him across the face, without any viciousness, then chuckled and drew back, well satisfied.

'How long did it take?'

'Exactly five minutes,' said Annie.

How long did what take? The drug, yes, but what drug?

'He's going to be a lump to shift,' said Sam, 'but we can fix it.' So they were planning to take him away; they didn't realise that Felicity and Beresford were watching, and the Flying Squad car was undoubtedly near the house; they weren't so good. But— what would they do when they knew that they were trapped?

Sam lit a cigarette, and blew smoke into Dawlish's face, while the woman stood up; she was old, she wasn't acting about that.

'Know what's happened to you, Dawlish?' asked Sam. 'You've had a dose of *curare*—heard of the stuff? It was once lethal, they used it in blow-pipes in South America. Now it's been refined and treated, and it acts on the muscles but doesn't affect the mind or the nervous system. We can do what we like to you, and you can't move. You can *feel*, though. And soon you'll be able to talk again. Then we're going to ask a few questions. If you don't answer pretty damned quick, you'll get hurt. We can do *anything* to you, and you won't be able to lift a little finger to help yourself. So you'd better talk.'

'He'll talk,' said the woman, walking across to the door. 'Not that we need much more from him. The big fool!' She gave the cackling laugh. 'He fell for it completely.'

'That's right,' said Sammy. 'Know what you fell for, Dawlish? We've known you were getting pretty close to the truth. We wanted you out of the way. So we fixed up for Kane to come and tell you about Geraldine Lorne's old servant—'

The woman's cackle sounded as if she were insane.

Sam chuckled.

'She's never worked for Geraldine Lorne or anyone in the family,' Sam said. He was gloating, but with complete lack of malice; seemed more amused by this development than by anything else. 'We knew you'd come if you thought there was any chance of finding Geraldine. We wanted to know exactly how much you *do* know. Annie's got a lot out of you—so the police suspect Geraldine of murder and of making her friends disappear! Just sit and think for a few minutes, Dawlish. Remember we want to know everything—and remember if you don't talk as soon as your tongue's loosened, we can cut you to little pieces. You'd feel it, but wouldn't be able to move an inch. Don't forget.'

'Sam, come and give me a hand!' called Annie from outside.

'Coming!' Sam gave Dawlish a mock salute, as if to rub in his last words, took his little finger and twisted; the pain was excruciating, but Dawlish could not even wince, could only sit and stare.

'We won't be long,' said Sam, and went out.

CHAPTER TWENTY-TWO

CAPTIVE

Ted Beresford saw the Rolls-Royce turn into the street off Clapham Common, and drove past the end of it. Felicity followed immediately afterwards, and as Ted stopped the car she drew up and hurried to him, looking round as she did so, as if in the hope that the police would already be at hand.

'We must find out the number of the house,' she said. 'Hurry.' She left Beresford, who could not get out of his car quickly, and crossed the end of the street—Friar Street; she saw that on a name plate which showed up beneath a street lamp.

She looked along the street.

The red light of the Rolls-Royce was stationary. She walked along the other pavement, and Kane, at the wheel, did not appear to look round. She caught a glimpse of Dawlish, standing in a doorway—the street lamp showed the cream paint, and she knew she wouldn't miss that house. Then the engine of the Rolls-Royce started up, and Felicity stood still abruptly; but the car only backed a few yards, away from the door.

Felicity drew nearer.

She heard Dawlish's voice, like a rumbling whisper, fancied

that she heard someone answering querulously; that conversation went on for a long time. Then the voices stopped, and the door closed. Felicity was then about twenty yards away. She saw a match flare and, in the glow, saw that Kane was lighting a cigar; he was preparing to wait.

Felicity went back along the street, and met Beresford at the corner; he hadn't rounded it, had not taken the risk of showing himself.

'Get the number?'

'No, but it's the house with the cream front door,' said Felicity. 'I think an old woman let Pat in. What do you think we ought to do?'

'Wait for him.'

'Doing *nothing*?'

Beresford said comfortingly, 'That's all he wants us to do—be around, in case anything goes wrong. He's pretty deep—if you need telling! He's pretty sure of what's at the bottom of this business, too, and—'

'He's not sure,' said Felicity emphatically. 'If he were, he'd have said so.'

'Don't agree. He would only say so if he thought it was going to help. While he thinks that hush-hush is going to serve a purpose, he'll keep mum. Don't we know Pat?'

'We know he wouldn't have asked me to warn the police if he didn't think he was sticking his neck out,' said Felicity abruptly.

'Nothing much can go wrong.' Beresford put a hand on her shoulder. 'Listen.'

They stood together, and the sound of a car engine sounded clearly; headlights swung across the common towards them, the car turned this way, and slowed down, then stopped a few yards in front of the Jaguar.

Trivett and another man came across, looming large in the

darkness. The driver sat at the wheel of the police car, and lit a cigarette. There was reassurance in his calmness and in the fact that Trivett had taken this call so seriously. There was always comfort in the knowledge that the Yard was at hand. Yet the darkness of the common, the bite of the wind, and the uncertainty of what Dawlish would find in that house, combined to make her reject easy assurance.

'What's it all about, Felicity?' Trivett asked, and there was an undertone of anxiety in his voice; there was whenever there seemed to be serious danger for Dawlish. 'Is he up to some fool game again?'

'Kane came and asked him to go and see an old woman who lives along Friar Street—in the house with the cream front door,' said Felicity, 'and he seemed to think that Kane was lying. I'm not sure he's right. He just asked me to tell you. He didn't stipulate any waiting period or anything like that, said we could leave it to the good sense of the police.'

'How long's he been here?'

'Ten minutes or so,' said Beresford. 'No sign of fireworks or bellows for help yet, and Kane is sitting near the house—'

'Smoking a cigar,' said Felicity, explosively indignant.

'We'll see what the place is like at the back,' said Trivett. 'Look after that, Smith.' The man with him hurried off. 'Does Pat think he's at the end of it?'

'He didn't say so. He said he thinks he knows what it's all about, but didn't say what.'

'Nothing else?'

'No.'

Felicity hugged her leopard-skin coat more tightly about her.

The men lit cigarettes, and they began to walk up and down in the chill wind. It was hard to feel reassured. After ten minutes, Trivett's man reappeared. There was a service alley leading to the back of all the houses in Friar Street, and a gate led from the back garden of each into the alley; so to make sure that no one came out, the alley should be watched at each end.

Trivett gave instructions, and as he finished, more police arrived and moved silently to their stations. Felicity began to feel a real easing of anxiety; there wasn't much chance of anything going seriously wrong, Pat had often taken bigger chances than this. As she walked up and down, with Beresford stumping along at her side, she felt a curious sense of well-being and of relief, due entirely to the fact that the house was surrounded.

Trivett hadn't said how long he would wait before he called at the house. One of his men had reported that it was Number 33, and the cream paint showed up beneath the street lamp; so did the Rolls-Royce. Occasionally they could even see the glowing end of Kane's cigar.

Half an hour passed.

Then the door of Number 33 opened, and a large man appeared. Felicity didn't actually see him; one of the waiting policemen did, from a distance, and called:

'He's coming out.'

Felicity hurried to the corner. By then, the large man whom everyone assumed to be Dawlish had walked the few steps from the front door, and was climbing into the Rolls-Royce. The light was poor, but Felicity recognised the cut of Dawlish's coat, and his hat. There was a mutter of voices, and Kane's cigar curved a red arc through the air, hit the pavement and gave off a shower of sparks, as the engine turned. Kane drove straight along, and through the rear window, Felicity saw the silhouette of both passenger and driver.

By then, Beresford was at the corner, with his car. Felicity ran to hers, but she didn't think that there was anything to worry about. Pat was probably going straight back to the flat. She hardly knew whether to be pleased or sorry; it looked as if the night's excursion hadn't worked out as he had expected, there had certainly been no general trouble, no need to raid.

Trivett climbed in and sat down heavily beside her.

'Pat couldn't be selling me a dummy, could he?' he asked suspiciously. 'I've no reason for thinking so, Bill.'

'Then his squib's misfired,' said Trivett. 'I'm leaving a man back and front, and when we've found out where Pat goes, I'll have a word with this woman myself.' He seemed as if he were uncertain about the wisdom of waiting so long, and didn't say what Felicity knew to be true—he was giving Pat another run for his money.

She still felt light-hearted.

Fifteen minutes after they had set out, and when they were on the Croydon road, Kane switched off all the lights of his car, swung off the road, and shook off his pursuers. That was the first time Felicity felt the need for fear, and it hit her fiercely.

The Rolls-Royce was found, parked in a side street, an hour later; there was no trace of Kane or Dawlish.

The man called Sam came back into the parlour at 33 Friar Street, smoking, swaggering; a man who was very pleased with himself. The old woman was outside, Dawlish could hear her pottering about. Sam stood with his feet planted in front of Dawlish and the one-sided grin on his lips.

'How're you feeling?'

Dawlish tried to answer; but his lips wouldn't move; it was like being fast in a nightmare. It held him in complete thraldom, and he knew a fear greater than any he had ever known. He couldn't move a muscle of any kind, anywhere; they could do exactly what they liked with him.

He tried to reject the thought.

Sam chuckled.

'I forgot, you're muscle bound and tongue-tied. That'll do you good, you're always talking too much. It'll be a couple of hours before you can talk again, and sometime to-morrow night before you can move. That's if you're still alive.'

His light voice made the threat sound even more sinister than it was.

'And you won't be, unless you talk,' said Sam. 'Now I've some news for you. Your pal Kane's driven off with another passenger. A big fellow, we hired him for the occasion, all we wanted was someone about your size to wear your coat and hat, and we couldn't use Kane, could we? Kane's driven him away. The police and your wife have gone careering after him, they think you're the passenger.'

Dawlish couldn't even think; but his nerves were raw, and he felt as if he were being suffocated.

'We knew you wouldn't come on your own,' said Sam, 'so we planned accordingly. Aren't we clever? There's a policeman back and front, watching. They'll both be fooled, Dawlish, because we're going next door. Through a door in the wall!' He chuckled again, seemed to be thoroughly enjoying himself. 'Then in the morning, you'll be wheeled out in a bath-chair, from next door. That's if the police are still watching. After that—'

He broke off.

'After that, he'll find Geraldine,' said the old woman from the door; and she cackled as she came in.

At half-past two, Trivett called at the house in person. The old woman, dragged out of her bed to answer the door, was more than querulous, she was spiteful. Yes, Dawlish had called to see her, talked a lot of nonsense about wanting to find a Geraldine

Lorne. She, the old woman, knew nothing about a Geraldine Lorne. The man called Dawlish had been almost offensive, hadn't gone for a long time. But as soon as he'd left she'd dragged her old bones up the stairs to bed, and she hadn't expected to be called out by interfering policemen. Why couldn't they leave her to live in peace?

Trivett hadn't any genuine excuse for searching the house. There was no apparent reason for thinking that the old woman was lying. Dawlish had left with Kane; and it was like Dawlish to make a sudden flight, to throw off the police; he might have decided that as he'd raised a mare's nest, it was best to work alone; he might believe that he could get more out of Kane if the police weren't around.

Trivett told Felicity.

Felicity had little to say; felt bleak and miserable.

Trivett called his men off Number 33 Friar Street.

At half-past nine next morning, Dawlish was wheeled in a large bath-chair out of Number 35 Friar Street by Sam; and Sam and the driver of a large Packard lifted him out of the chair and into the car. It was driven off immediately. He sat in a corner, limp and helpless; he had a severe headache, and his eyes were hot and prickly, but otherwise there was nothing the matter with him—except that he couldn't move a muscle.

He could talk, in a whisper; but only in a whisper, there wasn't a chance of raising a shout that might bring help. He sat well back in the car, and the blinds were half-down, so that he couldn't be seen by anyone who, by chance, might recognise him. Sam smoked and grinned, still on top of the world. The car went along a crowded main road, and all Dawlish could see were the legs and feet of the people on the pavement, the wheels and undercarriages of buses and cars, the lower parts of bicycles; it was as if half of the world had been cut away from him. The absolute helplessness to which he had been reduced made mockery of his physical strength.

They left the town, and drove through country roads; there was little traffic, and the car made good speed. Hedgerows, bare for the winter, the trunks of trees and field-gates, all flashed by him. Sam still kept the blinds down, although the risk of chance recognition was quite gone.

Dawlish hadn't the faintest idea what direction they were making, for the sun was hidden by heavy clouds; he had nothing to guide him. He almost lost count of time; he couldn't glance down to look at his wrist-watch and couldn't raise his arms to get the watch closer to his face. He tried to stop himself from thinking, but bitterness crept through; he had thought that by sending for the Yard he had made the night's adventure fool-proof. Foolproof!

He hadn't given the men credit for being expert kidnappers; they'd had much more experience than most.

The car slowed down, and changed gear, then turned a corner; he saw gates on either side. They were approaching a house, by a steep drive. The car had to change down again, because it was so steep, before the bottom part of the house came in sight; red brick, surrounded by neat-looking flowerbeds, all of them empty.

The car swung round towards a green front door, and then the driver pressed a button and the blinds went up.

Kane stood on the porch of the big, ugly house.

CHAPTER TWENTY-THREE

GERALDINE AGAIN

Sam climbed out before Dawlish, and looked at Kane; and although Dawlish couldn't see his expression, he judged from his voice that Sam wasn't pleased.

'Who let you loose?'

'Don't talk to me like that,' Kane said, and there was a rough edge to his voice. 'Is Dawlish here?'

'Sure he's here. Get inside, you'll see him later.'

Kane uttered a sharp expletive, but turned on his heel and went into the house. The door stood open. This was a large house, built at the worst period of Victorian architecture, of dull red bricks, with a slate roof and ugly windows. The floor of the porch was of red tiles, freshly polished, and there was no doubt that the place was lived in.

It couldn't be more than thirty miles from London, judging from the time Dawlish guessed they had been on the road.

The driver and Sam lifted him out; he couldn't stand by himself. A man wheeled a bath-chair from the hall, and it was bumped down the steps leading to the porch. They dropped Dawlish into it, then the three of them pushed the laden chair up the steps. It swayed from side to side, and Dawlish thought it would tip over, but they got it on to floor level at last, and wheeled him through the hall. This was spacious and well-furnished, with good taste. It needed only a swift glance at the oil-paintings, the panelled walls, and the oddments of furniture to tell that. A thick brown pile carpet clogged the wheels of the bath-chair, and it took two men to push him along a passage which was at the side of the stairs. Another door, leading to the back garden of the house, was chained and bolted; one on the right was open, and he was wheeled through it.

Geraldine Lorne and another woman stood in this room. It was charmingly furnished, obviously a woman's room. The colouring was pale yellow and light green; there were chrysanthemums in tall vases; a fire burned in a fire-place set in a corner. There were easy-chairs and a couch, all modern, all expensive.

Geraldine Lorne sat in one of them, and didn't get up, just stared at Dawlish with an expression which he couldn't understand; and just then, didn't try very hard. Hopeless? She had lost all the vitality and gaiety which had been so characteristic of her, her eyes looked heavy, as with sleep—or drugs? She sat back limply, and a thought flashed unbidden into his mind; that she was drugged in the same way as he.

Kane wasn't here.

The other woman stood by the fire-place, smiling at him. She was small, and she had a figure that rivalled Geraldine's. She was older—not much older, but getting on for thirty, he judged. Her hair was exactly the same shade as Geraldine's, and done in the same way, they wore identical clothes—dark-green frocks. They weren't alike, facially, but in their different ways each was lovely to look at.

The other woman smiled; and her smile reminded Dawlish slightly of the way Geraldine had smiled when he had first met her. It had something of the same charm, the same uninhibited freedom. She actually came forward and rested a hand on Dawlish's cheek, behaving in much the same way as Geraldine had when she had received him at Hailey Court.

'Good morning, Mr. Dawlish,' she said. 'I hope you've had a comfortable journey.'

Dawlish just stared at her; and Geraldine looked at him mutely.

'Of course, I'd forgotten you don't find it easy to talk,' said the woman brightly. 'That will soon pass, and—'

'He can talk,' said Sam, from behind the chair.

'Oh, can he? I hope he isn't going to sulk,' said the woman. She gave a little laugh, gay and youthful—too youthful, for her looks. Her size, the short dress, the way she did her hair, were all intended to make her look girlish; and actually robbed her of both grace and beauty and, to Dawlish, made her look a little foolish. 'It wouldn't do if we had to hurt him, would it, Sam?'

'I should worry,' said Sam.

She laughed again.

'You don't like Dawlish much, do you?'

'He's a pain in the neck. Ever since he played that trick on Rumbold—'

'Yes, I know,' said the woman. 'It upset our plans a little, Sam, but we haven't anything to worry about now. We have everyone we want, haven't we? Go and stay with Kane for a little while, and if he gets difficult—'

Geraldine started.

'Please don't—' she began, and her voice trailed off.

The other woman looked at her in pained surprise.

'You don't think we would hurt your Sebastian if it could be helped, do you, my pet? If he won't behave himself he'll have to be taught a lesson, but I think he's had enough lessons, by now. Off you go, Sam.'

Sam went out.

The woman stood in front of Dawlish, smiling down at him. She stretched out her right hand and stroked his cheek; he felt her fingers rasping gently over the bristles; there was a caress in her touch, she liked doing it; and that startled him. She laughed suddenly, as if she read and understood the expression in his eyes.

'Don't you like that?'

She drew her hand away—than slapped him across the face, a stinging blow; the diamond ring she wore struck against his chin, and cut. He felt it, swift and searing—it hurt much more than it would have, had he had a chance to move.

She drew back.

'Perhaps you liked that better,' she said. 'Now, Dawlish, I want to know *exactly* how much you've discovered or think you've discovered. And I'd like to know quickly, because I haven't much time to spare.'

The other woman gave a little moaning sound, as she looked at him; she had aged; she looked ten years older than when he had last seen her. The first woman ignored the sound, and peered at Dawlish. His utter helplessness filled him with a sense of rage and frustration; he couldn't even answer back, hadn't the proper control of his lips. He couldn't talk or bluff himself out of it, couldn't take advantage of any momentary relaxation. The woman had no gun; Sam had gone; yet she was as safe with him as she would have been with a new-born babe.

'Hurry, Dawlish,' she said swiftly.

Dawlish moved his lips slightly, made a husky sound in his throat.

The woman he knew as Geraldine Lorne jumped up, flung herself past the other woman, gripped Dawlish's hand and held it tightly, peered into his eyes, and begged:

'Tell her! Don't lie, don't pretend, tell her. She'll do such dreadful things, if—'

The other woman struck her across the face sending her reeling against the wall. Dawlish's hand fell helplessly by the side of the chair. The woman was a devil; anyone who looked into her blazing eyes then could tell it in a moment. Venom showed in them, although she didn't speak. Geraldine moved from the wall and went back to her chair, like a whipped dog.

'It was good advice,' the woman said thinly. 'Now, Dawlish, what do you *think* you know?'

He'd spoken a few words with Sammy, grunting them, and they hadn't sounded coherent; he didn't think he could string words together to make an intelligent sentence. He couldn't explain, he couldn't beg for time, could only watch the venom in her eyes and see her hands bunching at her side, ready to strike again. She actually started to swing her hand, but turned round, went to a work-box standing on a small table and picked up a pin-cushion. She took out a small pin, strode to him, and jabbed it into his cheek.

He couldn't flinch.

'Oh, please tell her,' sobbed the girl he knew. 'Please tell her.'

Dawlish managed to moisten his lips; it was an advance on anything he'd done before. He began to speak, in that unfamiliar, husky voice, as if he had an impediment; but his mind was working better, he knew exactly what he wanted to say and how to say it with the fewest words.

'She'—he glanced at the crying girl—'is not Geraldine Lorne. She impersonated—Mrs. Lorne.'

'Impersonated' sounded just like a jumble of thick sounds; would she understand them? He thought she did. Venom faded for a moment from her eyes, she gave a tight-lipped smile, and she was angry—coldly angry. It was even possible that her anger was tinged with fear. The pin was between her fingers, its threatened sting worse than a scorpion's. The words made the girl he knew sit up a little, and stop crying.

'How long have you known?' asked the woman.

'Since—yesterday.'

'Who else knows?'

That question spat out, obviously it mattered to her desperately. Had he been normal, had he been able to use his voice as a weapon, to taunt and tease and worry her, he might have had a strong position: but he could only force that husky monotone from his lips.

He could tell the truth: that no one knew. No one knew, because he hadn't been quite sure, although he'd felt amost sure. It was the one explanation which fitted everything; his Geraldine's fear and her uncertainties, the missing people—all people who had known Geraldine Lorne, and therefore all who could recognise her. Trivett had never suggested that he'd seen that possibility; he might be sitting on it. Felicity hadn't guessed, nor had Beresford. Dawlish had seen it, clearly, for some time now. The girl he knew as Geraldine was not really Geraldine Lorne. Suspicion had been slanted towards her, and she had been at Hailey Court so that if the police suspected she was behind the disappearances, they would strike at her. Whatever crime lay behind it, the girl he had known as Geraldine Lorne was only a stooge.

Kane knew, of course.

'Geraldine' had been kidnapped or else forced to come here, and Kane had been tormented by fear of danger to her; so Kane had deliberately let himself be used as a bait to catch Dawlish; a bait for this woman's use.

She was the real Geraldine Lorne.

She had the false Geraldine and Kane just where she wanted them; could use some form of compulsion, and did so ruthlessly. She had compelled the girl he knew to take her place.

She said softly, 'Who else knows, Dawlish?'

If he said 'no one', would she believe him? He doubted it. she would use pressure to make him tell the 'truth'. There was no telling just what she would do, but she would torture him; and he was an easy victim, mentally softened up. He hadn't the moral resistance he would normally have had, knew that while he remained like this, he couldn't fight.

'Who *knows*?'

She drew forward, with the pin stabbing towards his cheek again; it didn't quite touch.

Couldn't he fight?

Couldn't he try, at least?

He closed his eyes, and tried to slump down, as if he had lost consciousness. He didn't think his body moved at all, and his eyelids went down sluggishly; but they closed. He couldn't tense himself against what he knew was inevitable, but knew she would strike at him. The pin? Where? Her hand? Or would she think of some more vicious way to hurt?

Being unable to flex his muscles was agony in itself. He felt sweat breaking out on his forehead. He didn't know how long it would be—wasn't sure that she would strike at his cheek again. Perhaps she would go for his eyes.

He felt a prick, on his eyelid.

He heard a scream, a scuffle of sound, felt a scratch across the lid and then a shout.

'No!'

He heard heavy, laboured breathing and more scuffling. Now he had his eyes closed it wasn't so easy to open them, but he wanted desperately to know what was happening; to know how his Geraldine was faring; *his* Geraldine! That was a laugh, but there was no laughter in him, only a dread of what would happen to the girl.

His eyes opened.

He saw a blur of colour; the women's dresses and two hands intertwined; one was forcing the other back, the fingers were white where they were strained. His vision cleared, and he saw the two women locked together, *his* Geraldine holding the other's right wrist high above her head. The woman did not hold a pin, but a pair of scissors. Her lips were turned back, baring her teeth; it was ugliness itself. He could not see his Geraldine's face clearly, but could hear her gasping for breath; the other woman was physically stronger.

The woman holding the scissors had a tight hold on his Geraldine's left hand—she was forcing it back—so far back that Dawlish felt that bones would snap. He sat there, motionless, hearing everything, feeling the horror of it and with his help-lessness coming over him like the waves of an angry sea.

The two women were almost motionless now, but their arms and hands were moving in that terrible struggle. The scissors pointed downwards, as if *his* Geraldine were losing, because her strength wouldn't hold out. Suddenly she released her hold on the other woman's wrist—and the scissors swept downwards.

Dawlish groaned.

His Geraldine wasn't finished! She'd known what she was doing. She made a sudden convulsive movement, got her left hand free, and shot up both arms to meet the hand that was descending with the scissors.

Both women's bodies twisted. Light flashed on the scissors and they came down to breast level—and disappeared.

CHAPTER TWENTY-FOUR

SUSPENSE

Movement stopped. All Dawlish knew was that the light had glistened on the scissors, and then he couldn't see them. The hands of both women were at breast height. They stood like that for what seemed an age, and was actually only a few seconds; then his Geraldine gave a little moaning cry, and backed away.

She wasn't hurt.

The other crumpled up, and fell heavily. She fell on one side, and Dawlish saw the handles of the scissors in her breast; just the two loops for the thumb and finger, the blades were buried.

'Geraldine' stepped back, unsteadily, and stood with her eyes rounded and horror in them. The other woman made no move. There was no sound outside, and in the room only the faint noises from the fire; gas hissed from a lump of coal and sent a spurt of white smoke outwards; flame licked round the edges of the smoke.

'Geraldine' gasped; a moaning sound again.

From where Dawlish sat he could see the door and the window; there were wooden shutters folded back at the window, on the inside; a feature of houses of the period. The door was tall and solid; it looked like pine. The key was in the lock. Through the window, he could see a lawn and, on one side, a rose-garden, with the spiky bushes bearing a few withering leaves; and one or two flowers.

'Geraldine' said in a muted whisper, 'What shall we do?'

She turned to look at him, and he moved his lips, but only a faint sound came from them. He wanted to call her, wanted her to come and listen, but couldn't beckon, couldn't even move his head, to show her what he wanted. She looked back again at the other woman; and a red stain was on the dress near the point where the scissors had entered; the left breast.

He felt sure that she was dead; even if she were alive, she would be able to do nothing to harm them. He didn't think of her, but of this Geraldine and of himself. His eyes pleaded with her to understand, but she seemed as if she were dumbstruck; horror had paralysed her, much as the drug had paralysed him.

She took a step towards him.

'Yes,' Dawlish croaked. 'Come here.'

He didn't think she heard, but she came forward falteringly. He didn't know what strain she had endured during the past few days; but it was a great strain and had drawn the vitality out of her, set her nerves in twanging agony. She glanced down at the other's body several times in the course of a few steps, reached Dawlish and touched his hand—then clutched it tightly.

'What shall we do? They'll kill me, they'll kill you!'

'Listen,' he croaked; and his voice sounded louder.

She stared, as if she had understood and was hanging on his words.

'Lock—door. Put chair—beneath handle.'

She heard; she swung round and flew at the door. She made too much noise turning the key; if anyone were outside, they would hear. No other sound followed; why should anyone be outside, believing that he was quite helpless and sure that 'Geraldine' would not resist the other woman?

She came back.

'Yes?'

'Window—shutters,' he said. 'Fasten.'

She turned to the windows, started to unfold the shutters, hesitated, and turned and flew past him towards the door and switched on the light; she was beginning to think again. He found his lips twisting in a faint smile. She went back to the shutters, and after the daylight, this light was poor. Her hands were unsteady as she closed them. Bars fitted into sockets to keep them in place—one at the top and one at the bottom. She had to get on to a chair to secure the one at the top. When it was done, she jumped down and came towards him.

'Yes?'

'Search—room,' he said. 'Look for—gun.'

A light sprang into her eyes; hope? She turned and went to the bookcase, which had sliding doors at the bottom, opened them and rummaged among everything there. She didn't find the gun. She tried two drawers of a small, exquisite modern writing-table. The bottom drawer was locked, and she looked up helplessly. Dawlish could have forced it in ten seconds, with a knife which was in his pocket; she would probably take an age, even if she succeeded; and to break the drawer open would make too much noise. He didn't try to speak; there was nothing he could usefully say.

The girl moved suddenly, swift as a sprite, and picked up a handbag lying on a small table near the telephone. Dawlish stared at the telephone, but let her go on. She turned the bag upside down, and money, powder compact, lipstick, purse and keys fell out. She snatched up the keys and upset the compact; it opened; powder billowed about the room, and the scent reached him clear and sweet. She seized the keys and went to the writing-table, while he stared longingly at the telephone.

She opened the drawer, and exclaimed, 'Here's one!'

She took out an automatic pistol.

She didn't look as if she had any idea how to use it. Yet triumph still glowed in her eyes, and he wished he could show his approval. She needed no telling to come towards him, and he said:

'Telephone. Whitehall 12—'

'No, that's no use,' she said. 'There's a private exchange here, all the calls have to go through it.'

The telephone was just a mockery, a promise which betrayed him. He looked away from it.

'I can't use a gun,' she said.

He looked at the gun and she pulled up a pouf, but when she sat down, with the gun in her hand, he said:

'No. Drag—heavy—stuff—to—door.'

The chair she'd pushed beneath the handle would hold anyone up for a while; not for long. Was she strong enough to put really heavy furniture in front of it? She was up in a flash, no fool. She pushed two large arm-chairs towards the door, on their casters, turned them over and then heaved and pushed so that they blocked the door completely. Then she dragged the writing-desk over. She heaved and pushed it into position and he could hear her heavy breathing, but she didn't stop. When she had finished, perspiration had gathered on her forehead in little beads.

'Next?'

She asked the question as she looked round—and had an idea which brought another gleam to her eyes. There was a heavy metal fender; so heavy that she couldn't lift it from the floor easily. She dragged this across, and he watched her pushing it into position and saw the cunning with which she placed it, so that one side was against the wall, the other against a heavy chair; it would treble the strength of the barricade.

'There's nothing else we can do about the windows,' she said. Quite suddenly she seemed deflated. '*Is* it any use?'

Anything which gained five minutes was of use. Dawlish nodded, although she didn't seem convinced. She came over to him and sat on the pouf again, with the gun in her hand. Huskily, he told her how to open the magazine, in the handle; she did it at the second attempt; he was almost amused at the way she avoided the trigger. The gun was fully loaded; it would have seven bullets. He showed her the safety catch, and she shifted if off and on. He whispered:

'You need only slight pressure on the trigger. Hold it fairly loosely—not slack, not too tight. It'll jar your arm a bit.'

She nodded, but said, 'We're miles from anywhere, no one outside would hear a shot.'

He didn't speak.

'Sam's bound to come back, soon. He'll wonder why she's taking so long? He'll probably try to come straight in—or he'll knock, and if there's no answer, he'll suspect that something's the matter.'

'You'll answer,' Dawlish said. His voice was still only a croak, but he could talk more fluently. 'How does she usually speak to him?'

'Geraldine' hesitated, and then said softly, 'I'll send for you when I want you, Sam.'

It was a good imitation of the other woman's voice, too.

The other woman hadn't moved; in the fierceness of the past five minutes, Dawlish hadn't given her a thought. He felt sure that she was dead: the same thought was obviously in the girl's mind, for she moved, bent down and felt the other's pulse; then she dropped the limp arm.

'She's dead.'

She didn't speak, didn't look as if she were even mildly relieved—instead, she closed her eyes and swayed; he thought that she was going to faint. He sat watching her as she fought against the spasm, then bent down and, with set face, dragged the woman from the middle of the room, towards a corner. She stood a tall screen in front of her, so that she was partly hidden from sight.

There were two or three smears of blood on the carpet. 'Geraldine' averted her eyes, and came across to Dawlish. She was about to sit down, changed her mind and went towards the desk; there was a box of a hundred cigarettes, unopened. She opened it, lit a cigarette for herself, and offered him one.

He muttered, 'Can't smoke.'

He noticed nothing remarkable about that; and nor did she. She sat on the pouf and drew in the smoke, while he envied her—and then he started. He felt a slight movement; so light that it might have been imagination, but—he had shaken his head, he was getting some muscular strength back. He tried again; his head moved very slightly. 'Geraldine' stared at him, uncomprehending at first; and then she sprang up.

'You're getting better!'

'Quiet!' said Dawlish hoarsely; but his voice was stronger.

The flare of hope was good, while it lasted; putting new strength into them. It faded slowly; it might take hours for the strength to return properly, and they would not be able to stay here for hours, unaided.

There was no sound from outside. 'Geraldine' drew the pouf a little nearer and stretched out a hand, resting it on the back of his; but without suggesting that there was a sensuous caress behind the movement.

Her hand was hot.

'Sebastian can't come,' she said. 'Just before you came, Geraldine told me that he was to be drugged like you.'

'Tell me about it all,' said Dawlish gently.

She hesitated, looking at the glowing tip of the cigarette, and then said in a low-pitched, aching voice:

'She's my sister. I'm Elizabeth Steyning. I didn't see much of her, after she married Lorne. She was always—bad. I hate to say it, but she was. Men—oh, she was foul! I didn't want to live with her. We lived in South Africa for years. We've been orphans since we were quite young. I came to England because I hadn't any money, and she offered me a holiday in France and I took it. I was on the stage, but couldn't get anywhere. I met—Sebastian there. I didn't pay much attenton to him at first, he was all for her. We just got—got to know each other.

'Then—a man was killed. Murdered. She made it look as if I'd done it. She had evidence—finger-prints on a weapon. She told me to do whatever she ordered, and—I obeyed her. I lived in England for a while, as Geraldine Lorne. It gave her an alibi.'

Elizabeth Steyning paused, and looked past him; and her eyes were glassy, as if with hatred of the past and all the hurt it carried. Coals settled in the fire, but neither of them looked towards it.

'She tricked Sebastian, too. I don't know how—but she made him do what she wanted.

'Some time ago, she came to live in England. St. Albans. You've heard about that. I didn't go to see her there—I had to live in a little bungalow, near Worthing. I lived alone, had a few visitors—people she sent to stay with me, usually men who worked for her. Sam was one. I had to look drab, wear glasses. I couldn't understand why, for a long time. I thought it was just because she was jealous—she'd always said that I had the good looks. She wasn't—normal.'

The girl paused again, and Dawlish felt the tension in her grip on his hand. He didn't try to speak.

'Then, a few months ago, she told me to go and live at Hailey Court. I was to impersonate her, I'd had to make myself look a frump because Geraldine was at St. Albans, under her own name. She didn't want anyone to recognise me as Elizabeth Steyning. She told me exactly what to do. She told me a lot about her past life, so that I could answer questions if any were asked. She didn't tell me why, but I guessed she was in some danger and wanted to hide until it blew over. The only other living person who knew about it, I think, was Sebastian. He had to be a party to it. We didn't know what it was all about, until—until Sebastian discovered that several of the people she knew had disappeared. He was trying to find out what she was doing, why she wanted to pretend that she was someone else—and her secretaries had all gone. One of the men had, too. Nearly everyone who had known her in France and at St. Albans was gone; perhaps everyone, all those Sebastian tried to find were missing. You know—you know what he is. He told her about it—came here, and made a row. She told him that unless I maintained the impersonation, she'd use all the evidence she had against me and against him. And she told us why she was doing it.'

Dawlish's eyes burned with interest.

'She had some documents, records of a lot of her crimes, evidence to hang her—and they were stolen. She suspected her secretaries, and Moor and Hardy, then others. She started to kidnap the secretaries, one by one—none had it. Then she began on the men. Once she had them, she couldn't let them go. She'd taken the most likely thief first and worked down the list.'

Dawlish didn't try to speak, but full understanding came to him. It was so simple.

'Sebastian fought against it, I think if it had been just for himself he wouldn't have let it go on, but she had all those prisoners. And—he was desperately anxious to help me. Now and again, he seemed to lose his head, especially after I'd told him you had called. I was afraid he'd do something to get himself killed. Sebastian was always nervous about you, he'd heard a lot about you, and you were members of the same club. He acted well, that day he came to see you, but he couldn't keep it up. Then he decided to ask you for help, telling you part of the story.

'Geraldine discovered that, and frightened him. She frightens everyone. I had to act as I did with you, because there were microphones in my flat. Her men came for the tapes. If any was damaged she would have known. Sebastian searched but couldn't find them, and we agreed I'd have to act the part. It became almost natural.

'Then, Hardy came to see me—and Hardy knew the real Geraldine Lorne. If he'd caught a glimpse of me, the truth would have been out. Sebastian just lost his self-control, there was a dreadful fight. He told me about all this—I'd been taken away again then. But of course, you were there, weren't you?'

Dawlish nodded; and nodded again, and found that he could do so with greater freedom. He didn't try to interrupt the story, fought against letting hope rise too high.

'They'd taken me away the night before. The caretakers at Hailey Court worked for Geraldine, I had to go and stay in their rooms. She sent Sam to tell me what would happen if I let her down. Then he let me go back, the next morning I didn't dare tell Sebastian where I'd been—he might have smashed up the caretaker's place, and that would have been the end for us.

'She tried to kill Hardy. You know about that, too. When she heard that you'd saved him, she—well, she was worse than Sebastian at *his* worse. She knew that while Hardy was alive, she couldn't succeed in the plan, so she sent the caretaker to make me go downstairs again. They took me out, dressed as one of the boys in the maintenance staff, and I was brought here. She asked me if I knew how much you knew, whether you suspected. She was afraid of you, and began to plan to kidnap you, to make sure. She has this—dreadful drug.' Elizabeth Steyning shivered. 'She said all she wanted was to know the truth, but she wouldn't have let you escape. I was—frantic. If I tried to do anything, Sebastian would suffer. And—there was worse. Much worse really. These—these missing people. They're all here.'

That gave Dawlish his first real satisfaction—yet it was tinged with fear. He made himself ask:

'Alive?'

'Yes. So far. She hasn't found those papers, you see. She said that if Sebastian or I betrayed her, she would kill them all. I believed she would. We couldn't do anything. So Sebastian was used to fool you, he told me about that, too. She let us be together for an hour. They used that old woman, in Clapham. She talked to you, pretending she could help, while the drug took effect. It worked perfectly. Geraldine had told me so, so had Seb, but I didn't believe it until you came in. I thought you'd find some way out.

'Now—'

The girl paused and looked towards the screen, as if it failed to hide what she knew was there; the dead woman who had schemed this thing. So much was explained; only one big thing remained unknown—Geraldine Lorne's reason for doing all this.

The girl said slowly, with a kind of nervous hope:

'Are you feeling any better?'

He nodded again, and actually managed to lift his arm from

the chair; only an inch, and it quickly fell, but the use of his muscles was returning.

'If only we knew—' she began, and stopped, her hands flying to her breast.

Footsteps sounded in the passage outside. She stared at the door as if transfixed; and Dawlish was afraid, lest she wouldn't be able to answer if this were Sam and he called out.

The footsteps drew nearer, then stopped. There was a tap at the door.

'Want me?' called Sam, in his casual, confident voice.

CHAPTER TWENTY-FIVE

THE GUN

Elizabeth Steyning got up slowly, her whole body trembling. The gun was on the big pouf; she didn't pick it up, and Dawlish dared not speak to her. Her mouth was rounded, as if she were trying to speak but couldn't get the words out. Until then she had shown remarkable self-possession, but the shock of Sam's voice had robbed her of it.

Seconds seemed unending.

Sam's voice sharpened, 'Want me, Mrs. Lorne?'

'I—' began Elizabeth Steyning. 'I will send for you when I want you, Sam.'

There was a long pause; so long that it seemed to drag on for minutes; then Sam said:

'Sure, sure. Okay.'

He turned away and they heard his footsteps.

The girl dropped on to the pouf, and buried her face in her hands. Dawlish watched, compassionate and understanding; she had been so carried away by her story that she hadn't been ready for the call, hadn't been able to steel herself to it.

'It's all right,' he whispered.

It wasn't all right, and they both knew it. They had gained time, just a little time. There was no telling how long it would be before he recovered his physical strength, but there was little chance that it would come back in time. They were fooling themselves. Perhaps the girl had realised that, and it was partly responsible for her complete dejection. She didn't raise her head, just sat there hopelessly, with the gun at her side. Minutes passed, slowly.

'Tell me more,' Dawlish's voice was stronger, but he tried to stretch out a hand to touch her, and couldn't quite make it; yet he could lift his hand off the arm of the chair fairly easily. 'Do you know why she wanted you to take her place?'

'No. No.' The girl lifted her head with an effort, and her face was drawn and pale, her eyes were without hope. 'She—she just wanted to destroy all trace of herself. She was doing it, too. She—'

A thudding crash of sound broke across her words. The door shook and pictures shivered on the walls. The girl jumped to her feet and stood with her hands at her breast, staring at the door. Before she could speak, another thud followed; the door groaned and seemed to bend inwards, one of the chairs toppled over. A third, and the lock of the door smashed. The fender held it in position, but the rest of the barricade was pushed back a few inches.

Sam called harshly, 'Don't give me any trouble. Let me in.'

The girl stood like a statue.

Dawlish stared first at the door, what little hope he'd had completely gone. Sam had been suspicious, of course; he had pretended to be satisfied and gone away, and probably looked outside. The shuttered window had confirmed his suspicions, and he'd planned this battering attack on the door. He probably hadn't expected it would be so difficult to get down.

The girl gave a little, moaning cry.

'Don't make any trouble,' Sam repeated, and there was another terrific crash at the door.

Only the fender, jammed between chair and wall, prevented it from opening wide enough for the man to come in; but he could get an arm through now, a gun might poke round the corner at any moment.

Dawlish saw the automatic on the pouf.

It was only a foot away from his hand. He raised his arm and tried to lean forward; his back seemed to be locked. He gritted his teeth. He eased an inch from the back of the chair, the first body movement he had made since the drug had taken effect. He felt the veins standing out on his neck and forehead, and pain through his whole body. He stretched out for the gun, moving his fingers; he was only six inches from it.

Another crash seemed louder than the others, a chair toppled over, the fender scraped along the wall an inch or two. Elizabeth Steyning moved back, and turned and looked despairingly at Dawlish. He was gasping for breath, there was a dreadful pain at his chest.

The girl moved forward swiftly and picked up the gun, hesitated, and offered it to him. He took it and had a moment of dread, fearing that he would let it fall, but he didn't. He fell back in his chair, sweat running down his face, but the gun was on his lap, beneath his hand. He had sufficient strength in his fingers to handle it and shoot. The girl moved away.

The door burst open.

Sam and two other men rushed in; and Sam had a gun. He took the situation in at a glance, except one thing; he didn't see Geraldine Lorne. Dawlish recognised Parker as one of the other men; the servant who'd gone from the Hailey Court flat. He and the other men carried a long piece of timber which they'd used as a battering ram.

'Where—' Sam began, then his gaze roamed round, he saw the screen and his eyes dropped. He uttered an obscene oath, strode across to the screen, and pushed it aside. It fell against the wall.

He stared down at the dead woman.

Dawlish saw the muscles of his cheeks working, saw his hands clenching, as if the shock were physical. The man's perky self-confidence vanished. He moved slowly, shock and grief merged together and turned his face into a mask. He looked at Dawlish, then at the girl.

He said, 'So you killed her.'

He licked his lips, and shook himself, as if to throw off the shock. An ugly glitter replaced the blankness in his eyes. He moved towards Elizabeth Steyning, stretched out a hand and swung her round. She nearly fell.

'So you killed her,' he repeated. 'And I'll kill you. I'll kill you both.' He could hardly believe what had happened, but some colour was returning to his cheeks. 'You were the one she thought would always be easy. She could do what she liked with you, and you—killed her.'

Dawlish said, 'It was one or the other.'

His voice sounded surprisingly loud, compared with the hoarse whisper Sam had last heard. Sam turned to look at Dawlish, who saw the glitter in his eyes more clearly and sensed the hatred which the man was feeling.

'So it was one or the other,' Sam said in a choky voice. 'As if I didn't know! *She's* been on the spot for a long time.' He jerked his head towards Elizabeth Steyning. 'You're so smart, Dawlish, perhaps you know *everything*. Perhaps you know that Geraldine planned a suicide pact between Kane and Little Lizzie. Perhaps you know Lizzie was going to die, as Geraldine Lorne, and when Kane died with her, everyone who'd ever *known* Geraldine would be dead, *and* everyone who might have stolen those papers.

'Then she would come to life again—as Elizabeth Steyning. She would be protecting herself two ways.'

Of course; that was so obvious now. Dawlish didn't speak, didn't do anything to enrage the man, who seemed eager to talk as if it were a venom inside him which had to spurt out.

The girl stood like an image of stone. The other two men were near the door, watching; they didn't matter, they were simply part of the furniture.

Sam said in that harsh voice, 'It was all laid on. Geraldine was going to die, she'd be in the clear then. No one could ever catch up with her. She'd left her money to Elizabeth Steyning, so she'd have had it all right, and start again wherever she wanted to. It was brilliant. Understand, it was *brilliant*. Only Geraldine Lorne could have thought up anything like that. She traced everyone who could have taken the papers, and knew her well, and then she began to work it out. She caught everyone who mattered, except—Hardy. If we'd got Hardy the other night, it would have been over by now, and the right woman would have been dead.

'That's how much we owe to you, Dawlish.

'You didn't kill her with your own hands, but you killed her. If it hadn't been for you—'

He broke off, as if words were choking him.

Dawlish felt the steel of the gun beneath his hand; warm steel, now. He didn't move his fingers, for that would attract the man's attention. But he would get a proper grip on the gun, soon.

Would it be soon enough?

Sam said, 'She was always nervous of you, after she found out you belonged to the same club as Kane. She had the club watched. Had you watched, too. She was afraid there would be trouble. Then Trivett came to see you, and two of our boys were watching, one followed you, the other reported that your Scotland Yard pal was with you. The mistake she made was in letting you live.

'*I* won't make that mistake.'

Dawlish said, 'The mistake she made was in attacking Jeremy.'

'*I'm* talking,' Sam said. He stepped forward and smashed his fist into Dawlish's face. Dawlish's head went back, but he'd seen it coming, had been able to steel himself a little against the blow. He saw Sam leaning over him and glaring; he could feel the man's breath on his cheeks. '*I'm* talking, Dawlish. We killed Rumbold because he became dangerous. He let Jeremy follow him, made no attempt to get clear. He took Jeremy to the Soho hide-out, a place where Kane and I gave orders to small fry, but you could have got to places through Rumbold. We didn't take the chance of letting him take you. Geraldine had told Rumbold and the others what to say, if they were caught—they were to blame "Geraldine Lorne"—Little Lizzie. Lizzie would have been blamed for that, but she daren't have told the truth. We made sure she couldn't tell the truth, too, made sure she was watched all the time, we knew everything said in her flat. She just had to take it.

'But we couldn't catch Hardy. We daren't finish it until he was out of the way. We held the others—'

'You weren't so good,' Dawlish said. If only the girl would cause a distraction, so that he could get at the gun. 'The Parkers were working for you, and were shot out on their ears.'

'That's right,' said Sam. 'Lizzie had to be scared. Kane had thrown them out, and Lizzie soon wished she hadn't done it. Parker went back to make sure the microphone was working, and to put the fear of death into her. That was easy, it looked to you and Kane as if he'd gone back to take what he could find. He was just keeping the pressure up on Lizzie.'

Sam laughed; it wasn't a pleasant sound.

'Didn't you, Parker?' he asked.

The man by the door shrugged his shoulders.

Elizabeth Steyning moved suddenly, her hands still at her breast. She swayed, put out a hand to steady herself, and staggered across the room. Dawlish saw Sam turn towards her. Dawlish raised his hand off the gun, and held it in his fingers, and then covered it with his left hand.

'Where's Kane now?' he asked.

'Locked up, next door,' said Sam, 'and as helpless as you are. Mrs. Lorne drugged him herself. Know what I'm going to do, Dawlish? I'm going to set fire to the house. All the others are up in the attics. She was going to burn the place down when she got those papers, then stage the suicide pact with Lizzie and Kane. They'd be blamed, she'd be free. She was just waiting to get those papers, but I'm not going to wait. I'm going to do the job for her. You'll sit there unable to move, and you'll roast. Roast!' He roared the word, and then shouted at Parker. 'Get the petrol, start splashing it about.'

The two men went out of the room.

Sam turned to the girl, and said softly, venomously:

'As for you, Lizzie, I'm going to make you scream and writhe, I'm going to make you suffer for killing Geraldine Lorne. Understand? I loved Geraldine. I'd do anything in the world for her. I'd kill anyone who threatened her harm. I've been with her all the time.' He went to the girl but didn't touch her, and she cowered back against the wall. 'If it hadn't been for me, she wouldn't have realised there was any danger. She wouldn't have realised that one of her old boy-friends was after her. Tommy Moor—remember Tommy? He's upstairs, too. A friend of Tommy's got killed in France, remember? Suicide!' Sam laughed again, wildly. 'Suicide! Tommy didn't believe it. Tommy started to work to find out the truth about Geraldine. Tommy got it, too—he had enough to send her to the gallows, for murder, but he didn't have all the papers. There were enough to damn her, though, for drug-trafficking. He collected the evidence and kept it all in one place, and *I* went and got it.

'Then I snatched Tommy.

'He's had a bad time already, but it was a cake-walk compared with that you're going to get. Nothing can do Geraldine any more harm, so—'

He gripped the girl's wrist.

Dawlish shot him, through the head.

The shot rang out loudly, and would be heard in the rest of the house—or most of it. Where was Parker? Where was the other man? If they were in the attics, splashing petrol about, they might not have heard.

No one came.

The girl stood against the wall, chalk-white; there was no strength in her. Sam lay at her feet, with blood oozing from the hole in his temple.

Dawlish put his hands on the arms of the chair, gritted his teeth, and made a great effort to stand. His back seemed to break in two again, but he managed it and stood upright. He supported himself with one hand against the chair for a moment, then let it go. He took a step forward. It was a shuffling step, but he didn't lose his balance.

Could he stop them firing the house?

Could he hope—

He heard a crash, not far away, then a bellowing voice, another crash—and the voice sounded louder.

The girl cried out, 'That's Seb, he's got out!'

CHAPTER TWENTY-SIX

PARTNER IN CRIME

Only Sebastian Kane seemed to be able to put any life into her. Her pallor remained, but she moved away from the wall, passed Dawlish, and reached the doorway. She disappeared. Dawlish took another step, but knew he couldn't make the door without help.

He stood still, feet planted wide apart.

The girl cried, 'Seb, be careful, there are men upstairs. They're going to set fire to the house, there are a lot of people in the attic.'

'*What's* that?' Kane demanded.

'Seb, you've got to stop them, you—'

'I'll stop them,' roared Kane. 'Their damned drug couldn't put me out, so nothing will?'

Obviously he thrust her aside, and Dawlish heard him thudding up the stairs; there was no other sound. Dawlish tried to call out loudly enough for the girl to hear him, but she didn't come back. Was she following Kane and taking a desperate chance?

The sounds faded.

There was a long silence, broken abruptly by the girl's

footsteps. She reached the door. She looked better—haggard and drawn but with some colour in her cheeks, the paralysing numbness gone. She even managed to smile as she came to Dawlish, put an arm round his waist and, absurdly, supported him back to his chair.

'I've telephoned the police,' she said. 'They'll be here soon. I—I'm going to help Seb.'

'No! You stay—'

She pressed his hand, and went towards the door, but she didn't need to go far. Sebastian Kane thundered down the stairs, roaring her name; and he still called her Geraldine. They must have met at the foot of the stairs.

'That's fixed them,' roared Kane. 'They didn't see me coming, I broke one man's neck. Parker's! The other won't be much use for the next few months. And everyone's all right up in the attic, they're coming down. Just came to check on you, I'll go and help them.'

Dawlish heard the smack of a kiss.

Dawlish did not smile.

The house was near Horsham, and the local police arrived twenty minutes after the call. They took over immediately, and the prisoners, none of them seriously hurt, were given food and drink. Dawlish knew little about that. He sat in a small room, where two policemen had carried him, alone most of the time. He was getting the power of movement back again, and could ease forward in his chair without difficulty. The weight of dread was gone, but there was another weight—great compassion for Elizabeth Steyning.

She believed now that she knew everything.

He was still thinking of her when he heard new arrivals. Trivett? He heard voices, including the Yard man's, but it was some time before Trivett came into the room.

Dawlish forced a grin.

'Hallo, Bill. Told Fel about this?'

'Of course.' Trivett stood in the doorway, looking at him anxiously. 'How are you? They say you can't move.'

'That's wearing off,' said Dawlish. 'I'll be fine. How much do you know?'

'Most of it, I think. I've seen Kane and the girl, they've told me pretty well all that matters. I've seen the man Moor, too—he'd set himself out to bring Geraldine Lorne to book. She'd already conceived this fantastic scheme. In all, eleven murders. When she despaired of getting the documents she'd lost, she was going to become her sister. The influence she had over people must have been fantastic to keep Kane and Elizabeth Steyning quiet—'

Kane came striding into the room. The girl was just behind him; looking much better.

'Someone talking about me?' Kane boomed.

'Yes,' said Trivett. 'Not all to your credit, either. I can just understand most of it. I can understand Miss Steyning being coerced into doing what she was told, but you—I can't understand you letting it happen.'

Kane coloured furiously.

'I wonder what you'd do, in the same circumstances,' he sneered. 'I wanted just one thing, to save the woman I loved.' He put his great arm round the girl. 'I'd go through fire and water any day of the week to help her. And—'

'But you weren't helping her,' Trivett said. 'You were making it worse for her.'

'You're crazy. Policemen! No wonder—'

Dawlish said softly, 'He's not so crazy, Sebastian. You were making it worse for her, all right, and you knew it.'

Kane glared at him, and took his arm away from the girl.

'Mr Dawlish—' she began.

'Just a minute, Miss Steyning.'

Trivett was abrupt.

Dawlish still held the automatic in his right hand, covered by his left. He looked straight into Kane's eyes, and thought he read understanding in them.

'You knew it, and you did it deliberately,' he said. 'Your job was to keep so close to the pseudo-Geraldine that you knew every move she made. You pretended to be understanding and helpful and in love, but you weren't, Seb. If you cared for anyone, it was for the real Geraldine Lorne, but it didn't go very deep.'

'You're—mad!' said Kane.

His voice was surprisingly thin and reedy.

'Think so? You foxed and fooled me at every turn. You asked for help, then rejected it, kept confusing the issue. You were keeping yourself clear while you did all that. You were in a perfect position to sit on the fence. To get Elizabeth's confidence completely, you slung the Parkers out, because she began to suspect them, but Parker had to come back for one or two tape recordings he'd made secretly—sweet Geraldine didn't really trust *you*. While pretending to be so concerned for Elizabeth, you were working to get her caught more tightly in the web.'

Kane's lips were set, and he breathed heavily through his nostrils.

'You lied right and left about Annie Mellor,' went on Dawlish. 'But you always played your hand so that you seemed to be full of ferocious goodwill. You were with sweet Geraldine body and soul—for just as long as it paid you.

'You were in the next room here. That drug would have worked, if you'd taken it. You hadn't—so Geraldine said she'd given it to you, but she hadn't. You heard everything that Sam said to me, and learned Geraldine was dead. By then, Seb, you'd touched the bottom of corruption. You'd had plenty of time to think it all out, you always feared you might not be able to get away with it. So you carefully laid everything on, so that you seemed to be one of the victims. When you decided the main scheme wasn't practical, you changed horses. You'd be sitting pretty, for you'd marry Elizabeth, who'd probably get her sister's money. Wasn't that it, Seb?'

No sound came from Kane but the heavy breathing.

'You then decided that you would appear as the great hero, rescuing everyone who was in distress,' Dawlish went on. 'You plotted it all with Geraldine, but kept an escape route open. Sam didn't know you and Geraldine were in it together. He wouldn't have stood for that—he was in love with Geraldine. You and Geraldine were planning a suicide pact all right— between *Sam* and Elizabeth. You both fooled him, but you were always prepared to rat on Geraldine. And you took that evidence against her, didn't you?'

Kane's eyes were glittering.

'Then Elizabeth did the biggest job for you,' Dawlish went on.

'When she killed Geraldine in that struggle, you had only one more job to do—put up a good show. Sam believed you were one of the victims, Geraldine had had you put in the next room, kept separate from the others because of this phoney suicide pact with Elizabeth. Sam thought you were helpless, but not you.

'You knew the moment that I'd dealt with Sam.

'You broke out and put on your final act, but it didn't work, Seb. I'd placed you as a liar and a cheat from the beginning. You were once so completely dominated by Geraldine Lorne, and now supposed to be passionately and doltishly in love with Elizabeth. When I realised there were two women, not one, your part just didn't fit. You never seemed natural when with Elizabeth—but you put up a nice act.

'How do you like my version, Seb?'

Dawlish finished.

Kane didn't speak.

Elizabeth Steyning said gaspingly, 'It can't be true!'

'Can you prove this, Pat?' Trivett asked sharply.

Kane stared—but kept silent.

'Oh, yes,' said Dawlish, smiling. 'There isn't a shadow of doubt, Thomas Moor discovered that Kane and Geraldine were working together. I discovered that from Moor's wife, when I went to see her. Sam stole all the evidence Moor had found, except that, and—'

Kane, resistance broken when he believed that the truth was known, leapt at him, great arms raised.

'I'll kill you first,' he roared. 'I'll kill you as I killed the others. I'll choke the life out of you!'

Dawlish shot him, in the knee. He crashed down in front of Dawlish, pain driving the rage out of his face.

'Why the devil didn't you give me the proof that Moor had about Kane?' demanded Trivett. 'If you'd told me that at the time—'

They were alone.

Dawlish grinned, broadly.

'Oh, William! When will you know that I can't tell the truth if I'm paid to? Moor hadn't any proof—certainly his wife hadn't. It was the one thing which I thought would make Kane crack, he couldn't know it wasn't true, and it just did the trick. You've his confession now, haven't you? Even poor Lizzie will swear to that. You'll find that stuff Geraldine wanted at his flat or at his room at the club.'

Trivett didn't say a word.

He found the evidence against Geraldine Lorne in Kane's safe.

* * *

Three weeks later, Tim Jeremy left the hospital, convalescent but with no permanent injury. He was to spend a few weeks at Dawlish's Haslemere home, but went first to the flat. There, because he had been permitted a measure of excitement, many were waiting to welcome him, including some who had not seen him before. The Hardys—for they were married —Millicent Green and Elizabeth Steyning, and of course Beresford and the Dawlishes.

Kane had been committed for trial; the others who had served Geraldine Lorne were also awaiting trial. Annie Mellor had made a confession as full as it could be, the weight of evidence against Geraldine Lorne, for crimes steeped in corruption, was overwhelming; and most of it could be used against Kane. The defence might claim some clemency because so many of her victims had been found alive. In fact, her plan to hold the prisoners had been much less risky than killing them one by one; the bodies would have been found. Loretta Mannion, last of the secretaries to be kidnapped, had been hidden in the caretaker's rooms at Hailey Court. She had escaped, and the caretaker had to kill her to prevent her from being caught. Sam was with him at the time. The only handy hiding-place for the body was the flat—they used the service lift. While he was looking for something to put the body in, Dawlish arrived. The caretaker had rescued the man Dawlish had put in the alcove, too.

Geraldine had loved Kane, but had needed Sam; so she had been careful to make Sam think she was going to kill Kane. The real truth about Parker's visit came out in that evidence; Sam had sent Parker to the flat, in the first place. Kane shot him out, partly to annoy Sam, partly to please Elizabeth. Sam sent Parker back, to check on the microphone, and Kane had been so surprised, at seeing him, that he had blurted out his name.

Only Elizabeth Steyning grieved, bitter though she must have felt. Kane had tried so cunningly to frame her, even when telling Dawlish that she had known what had happened to Rumbold.

She had stayed at the flat for the past three weeks, and Dawlish believed that she was going to throw off the effects of the shock fairly quickly. She was to take Hilda's place, sharing a flat with Millicent Green. She had a great inheritance and had talked of not wanting to handle the money, whereupon Felicity had talked, earnestly, about the possibility of doing good with it, and made her point.

Hardy's man was out of danger, but still in hospital.

The Moors were together and, if Dawlish judged rightly from his two visits, likely to be a most contented couple. Only Loretta Mannion had died, of those who had known Geraldine Lorne well.

'Taken by and large,' said Tim Jeremy, when they had chatted for an hour, 'no one should grumble. Not even you, Lizzie!' There was sympathy and understanding in his eyes as he looked at the girl. 'Thank your stars for a lucky escape—or am I putting my clumsy foot in it?'

'You are,' said Felicity.

'You're right, of course,' said Elizabeth, and smiled—almost as gaily as when Dawlish had been to see her at Hailey Court, when desperation and fear of a hidden microphone had forced her to act the part of Geraldine Lorne with superb naturalness. 'Don't think I'm going to brood over it, any of you. I wish he weren't going to be hanged, I shall hate the trial, but—'

She broke off.

She would never forget Kane: but in a few months it would not hurt so much.

ABOUT THE AUTHOR

John Creasey, born in 1908, was a paramount English crime and science fiction writer who used myriad pseudonyms for more than six hundred novels. He founded the UK Crime Writers' Association in 1953. In 1962, his book *Gideon's Fire* received the Edgar Award for Best Novel from the Mystery Writers of America. Many of the characters featured in Creasey's titles became popular, including George Gideon of Scotland Yard, who was the basis for a subsequent television series and film. Creasey died in Salisbury, UK, in 1973.

THE PATRICK DAWLISH MYSTERIES

FROM OPEN ROAD MEDIA

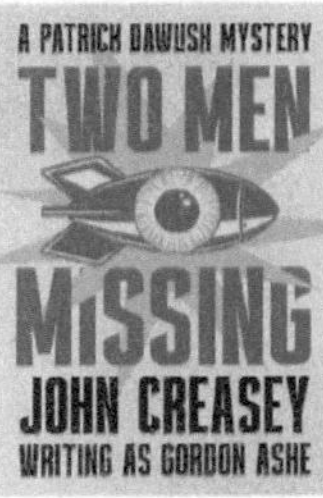

EARLY BIRD BOOKS
FRESH DEALS, DELIVERED DAILY

Love to read?
Love great sales?

Get fantastic deals on bestselling ebooks delivered to your inbox every day!

Sign up today at
earlybirdbooks.com/book